Nuala

Nuala

KIMMY BEACH

A FABLE

THE UNIVERSITY OF ALBERTA PRESS

Published by

The University of Alberta Press
Ring House 2
Edmonton, Alberta, Canada   T6G 2E1
www.uap.ualberta.ca

LIBRARY AND ARCHIVES CANADA
CATALOGUING IN PUBLICATION

Beach, Kimmy, 1964–, author
    Nuala : a fable / Kimmy Beach.

(Robert Kroetsch series)
Issued in print and electronic formats.
ISBN 978–1–77212–296–1 (softcover).–
ISBN 978–1–77212–308–1 (EPUB).–
ISBN 978–1–77212–309–8 (Kindle).–
ISBN 978–1–77212–310–4 (PDF)

    I. Title.
II. Series: Robert Kroetsch series

PS8553.E119N83 2017   C813'.6
C2016–907976–7   C2016–907977–5

First edition, first printing, 2017.
First printed and bound in Canada
by Houghton Boston Printers,
Saskatoon, Saskatchewan.
Editing by Helen Moffett.
Proofreading by Meaghan Craven.

A volume in the Robert Kroetsch
Series.

The University of Alberta Press is
committed to protecting our natural
environment. As part of our efforts,
this book is printed on Enviro Paper: it
contains 100% post-consumer recycled
fibres and is acid- and chlorine-free.

The University of Alberta Press
gratefully acknowledges the support
received for its publishing program
from the Government of Canada,
the Canada Council for the Arts, and
the Government of Alberta through
the Alberta Media Fund.

She loves me the moment Seeing-Servant pulls the cables and opens her eyes for her. She is mine and I am hers.

She asks me, 'Why am I called only Nuala? I knew my name when I awoke, but why am I not called Nuala-Servant if you are called Teacher-Servant?' I tell her it is because she is not a Servant as I am. Nuala is 'She Who Is Served.'

She only woke yesterday. Today I shall give her all of her names so that she may become used to them. I shall call her Nuala, as she calls herself. I shall call her beloved. Little one. She will grow accustomed to me calling her when I want her attention. When I wish to teach her of her Giant nature.

I opened her eye, and she found me watching her. My eyes looking into the fire of her left eye. She gave me the gift of her first gaze, and it shook me to my viscera how quickly she understood this gift. We now transcend, spiralling in the liquid realm of thought-talk. She will not speak, for she cannot. But I may speak to her. From this moment, her thoughts and mine will become one.

When she stands for the first time, she will learn that if she wishes to see me as I tread the ground, she must look down; and I must tilt back my head, expose my throat to the wind, look up to meet her eyes. Her clear, seeing eyes, though only a day old. She will see that she is Giant and I am He Who Is Not Giant.

Today,

we transport Nuala from the City of Servants to her new home in the Great City. We have been gradually furnishing our city rooms with objects we love best, though none of us was certain we would be chosen. Our goodbyes from those left behind—those not chosen for the Service—were necessarily swift, heartbreaking.

My lodgings are small and comfortable and I shall do my best to feel at home, for Nuala's sake. My books are here. The cloth ribbons are here: those with which my mother once tied back my hair, her hands pushing through the long strands of it, taming it inside fabric. These shall bring me solace in the inevitable periods of loneliness to come.

We roll the great bed into the streets of the city. Seeing-Servant's cables open Nuala's eyes, and Head-Servant turns her head first to the right and then to the left. Her blonde hair tumbles either side of her Giant pillow.

'Look around you, little one. Soon we will walk together through these streets and have adventures such as you could never dream.'

'Oh, Teacher-Servant. What is *walk*? What are *adventures*?'

'Patience, my love. Soon you will know all. And I have the honour of teaching you.'

We move among the small people who will soon look up as she strides through their streets among their movings and doings. Word of Nuala's waking has spread through the Great City, and crowds are gathered in front of brick and limestone to watch her pass by on this, the second day of her life. Some of her citizens throw flowers upon her bed: a welcome to the new Puppet Queen. Others have knitted scarves for a metal throat, and mittens for Giant hands. Some have been stitching for years, making a Giant-sized quilt they feared they would never have the chance to present. They have let it blow and toss in cool wind for the last two days, to make sure it is fresh for Nuala's bed.

A long line of citizens approaches with the rolled-up quilt. Ten Clothing-Servants and Iron-Servants climb ladders up to the mattress upon which Nuala lies, awake and seeing. The quilt-bearers pass it up to the Servants, who unroll it and lay it over Nuala's body. Bold and proud flowers, panels of silk and cotton, some blue, some red.

My fellow Servants—most of whom I have known since childhood in the City of Servants—shake my hand, clap the shoulders of my new uniform, place shy kisses on my cheek. At long last, we are able to give full voice and heart to the blessings we have practiced on one another since we were children. The hopes we wished one another each time we met. The words were rote, then. Now, they burst from our mouths. We sing them into the cool morning air: 'May our joy be trebled in the Service!'

I take my tea in the damp morning air outside my new lodgings. I am eager to don the unfamiliar grey Servant uniform I must wear, for it signals the beginning of my service to Nuala.

How quickly Nuala is mine. How quickly my heart is thrust into the core of her oak and brass. I am keenly aware that had she not given me the gift of her first gaze, she would have chosen another as her Teacher-Servant. My good fortune!

How my insides tumbled and burned when she chose me. I am still light-headed and giddy with the joy of it. The gift of her first gaze is a bliss transcending all other moments in the Service. A mass of exploding light pouring out my fingertips. I am the first in common memory to feel this breathlessness, this unfolding of love. I curl my hands inward and hold it deep inside of me. It is mine and mine alone.

The tea is sweet and thick. I make notes. How delicate her new hands seem. The Wrist-Servants and Walking-Servants must examine, assess, and attach her joints to the cables that will support them. But all gently.

The great bell tolls, its clapper free to swing again after such a long interval, its proud heralding of morning, the awakening of Nuala. She wakes early, and I must be ready when she does.

Seeing-Servant will not open Nuala's eyes until I am at her side. Until I am looking into her eyes. I must always be the first Servant she sees.

Her deep green eyes take in the length of me and settle on my face.

Never have I been so observed! Her eyes pull my heart to the limits of my chest. Her eyes. They dip into the paint of my body. She paints a picture of me in her mind, her lashes the brush that spreads the colours of my arms and torso, the brush with which she will render my likeness inside her head.

'Good morning, my beauty.'

From the pocket of my grey tunic, I produce the tube of fragrant oil I work into the delicate hooks and eyes at her lids. The brush and whisk of the fine lashes against my forearms, my hair rising in response. Then the fall and curve of her throat. The welded metal and nails holding her mouth closed. This last shall not open again, and yet it must remain oiled. My beloved need never fear rust. She feels me lubricate her neck. Feels me climb next to her on the pillow to oil the hook-and-eye assemblies above her ears and atop her blonde head.

Head-Servant has arrived from his resting place and positions himself behind the great ball of Nuala's skull, ready to lift. Even though her eyes are fully open and seeing, she is groggy with sleep. I look inside her thoughts to the milky lingerings of what was her first dream. Her mind twitches, needing to share with me the strange pictures she has seen there. Her thoughts recoil, and I see into the wildness of her eyes.

'Shh, my Nuala. I am with you. Today I shall teach you the newness of you.' Her breathing slows at my voice, her visions stilled by my words.

'Do not believe the pictures in your sleeping head, Nuala. They are not true. Between the time you go to bed and the time we share now, you lying down and me looking upon your innocent eyes, we sleep, and during those sleeps, we dream. Were you to tell me of each one, my child, we should have no time to speak of anything else.

'We may dream of being in another city, or we may dream of somewhere that exists only in our time of sleep. We may dream of being unable to move, Nuala. I saw your dream. No other Giants can harm you or take you from me. No other Giants shall cause you to be immobile. Do you understand? I will ensure that you can always move. I am yours, and you are mine. This shall ever be.'

'I am yours and you are mine. This pleases me, Teacher-Servant.'

The Engine is quiet for the moment. The pulleys have been tested, the wires and hooks are connected and secure. We wheel her bed from her sleeping place, and uncover her under the early morning sun.

'Soon you shall be clothed in a pretty red dress, little one. Would you like to see it?'

A 'Yes' flickers from her thoughts to mine. 'But first, you will need to shower in warm water. Would this please you?'

'Oh yes, Teacher-Servant. I would like to feel what you call water upon me.'

Two Engine-Servants bring the Engine to life, and steam hisses in its belly. Head-Servant helps raise the globe of Nuala's skull. The Engine pulls her head up slowly. It stretches its long arms over Nuala, and lifts, lifts her until she is seated, her legs over the edge of her bed, the sun casting long, shivering shadows of cables on her face. Clothing-Servants undo the great buttons at Nuala's back and pull the nightgown from her air-cooled arms. A ribbon at the gown's sleeve catches the hook above her wrist. Clatter of her hand from her lap to the bed beside her. 'Careful. *Careful.*' These clumsy Servants!

Then it extends the red metal lizard that will snake into Nuala's lower back to keep her upright and steady.

I pull the long ladder out from under her bed and rest it against her child-hip. 'What is that you climb me with?' Nuala asks me, alarmed by its long and spindly legs.

'It is simply a ladder, one which I will use each day to reach your shoulder and which your Servants will use to take care of you. Remember its shape, for it will never harm you.'

I pull soft grey slippers from my uniform pockets, remove my shoes, and place the felt slippers upon my feet. This is my Walking-Upon-Nuala footwear: that which I don to tread on the hard shoulders and unyielding lap of my beloved.

I pull the ladder up behind me and lay it against her child-breast. Up I crawl to sit on her left shoulder, my hands inside her hair, my own long locks tickling her earlobes as I kiss the whorls of her inner ear.

The iron serpent unfurls and stretches toward her back. Below me, a Walking-Servant parts the curtain of fabric that covers the tender opening at Nuala's lower back, its maw awaiting the Engine's stabilizing mechanism.

I whisper her this: 'A beautiful wooden girl woke one morning to find that the world she knew was much changed. Instead of being surrounded by the tiny people of the Great City as she was used to, she now found herself in the company of Giants. Some could look down upon the small Giant, and others, younger even than she, looked up at the young Giant. Some were as tall as the tallest of trees at the edges of the young Giant's city.'

'What are *trees*, Teacher-Servant?' Nuala asks. She does not feel the pincers of the Engine's great fist as it wraps itself around her spine.

'They are tall beings, my Nuala. As tall as you, and some taller. Trees are fixed to the earth and may not move, but they love and breathe as you and I do. One day we will see the trees together, and soon, I will show you a picture of a tree. For now, do not fear what you do not know. I will teach you. Patience, my Nuala.

'The other Giants cherished the young one. They embraced her and called her Our Beloved. She was pleased to be among so many Giants, among those of her own kind.'

I tell her of other Giants, and of the great trees, and while I speak, Head-Servant attaches the clasps to the metal loop atop her head, and to the clamps on either side of her face, so that she may turn her head and gaze upon the city's tiny people, who will want to walk with her. The new living Giant for whom we all have waited the length of our lives.

The Engine lifts Nuala and sets her feet upon the soft cloth I have laid on the ground outside her room. A long spigot extends from the Engine's great arms, and expels warm water over my Nuala's head. Seeing-Servant closes her eyes so that water will not run into them. I open my umbrella, my hand on her ankle, so that she will feel me and not be afraid. The water pours over her, pours down her knotted throat, the pine and rosewood of her. Runs from the edge of her finger-tips and over my umbrella. Huge drops reach the earth and soak my legs. Water ricochets from the ground, drips from her knees and soaks my arms and torso. I toss the umbrella aside. Why not be as wet as she? I step back dripping, and vow to forget my umbrella for the morning showers. I look up at her through the warm water falling from her thighs and wrists, to feel the cascade as she feels it. An ant in the splash of a heavy raindrop from the tallest reaches of pine.

'I like this feeling, Teacher-Servant. It is as though all of me is moving. What is this called?'

'It is called a shower, my love, remember? And you shall have one every morning.' I remove my soaked tunic and hand it to my best friend, Senior Iron-Servant. She will dry it for me. It is chilly, but I do not feel the cold. Bare-chested, I climb the Engine and crawl over the long arms holding up her head. I hold the rope ladder designed for this purpose and the Engine lowers me so that I am hanging before my beauty's face. Other Servants lean ladders of varying lengths against her legs and hips. They climb her knotted surfaces, towels at the ready to dab beads from her thighs and wrists. Only I am permitted to touch her eyes, her cheeks. Touch the soft towel to the slope of her nose, the rigid pout of her lower lip.

Seeing-Servant has opened Nuala's eyes so that she may see me work about her face. A fat drop from an eyelash lands on me. Its warmth courses across my forearm. My fingers brush the water from around her eyes. Her gaze shreds me; her attention crumples me. I am reflected in the glass of her eyes. Seeing-Servant closes them so that I may wipe the water from the lids.

'Where are you, Teacher-Servant? I cannot see you.'

'But you may feel me. And this is my scent.' I hold my long hair under her nose and rub it between my fingers to release the fragrance. 'Remember it. It is always I who shall gather your hair to wring the water from it. Always my strong arms that will shield you and wipe the drops from your eyes.'

'I think that this is the reason you have hands, Teacher-Servant. To place them in my hair, to sweep the water from my face.'

In the mornings, before dawn and while Nuala sleeps, the Iron-Servants gather in their workshop.

In this bustling room stands a table many feet wide and longer still. Laid out on it before the Servants is Nuala's red dress, which two dozen Iron-Servants have laundered and will now press. They wear grey suits as we all do, but theirs are lighter, as their work is hot and strenuous.

My insides thrill watching the Iron-Servants work. The dress had lain so long in a musty trunk. It required a thorough wash, an airing, and a tuck of the hem so the dress could fit a Giant as small as Nuala.

The room sweats despite the fans and the long, low, open windows that usher in the spring winds and allow the Iron-Servants to see out into the street and watch the people their own size: those not in the Service. Cordial greetings pass through the slanted panes. 'Joy to you, Citizen!' calls an Iron-Servant into the lightening street. 'And to you, kind Servant!' comes the reply. 'May your joy be trebled in Nuala's Service!'

Many ironing stoves stand ready, each with four sadirons upon it. I long to help, to feel the warm cotton in my hands, but the Iron-Servants have perfected their task, and although they are too kind to say it, my *help* would be hardly that.

I was a lithe and small boy in the City of Servants long ago, peppering my best friend, the future Senior Iron-Servant, with sunrise questions. 'Why are these irons called *sad*? What makes an iron sad? I did not know that anything but we could be sad.'

She laughed at me and explained that neither the irons nor the future Iron-Servants were sad. Did I not notice the joy with which they performed their morning duties, even though there was then no Giant to wear the dress they tended? It was simply the name given to the heavy slabs of metal.

'Why is a tree called a tree, my son?' The question had me reaching for days, reading books and finding answers. I learned that the *sad* in *sadiron* was a form of the old word *sald: solid.*

I ran to the great ironing room to tell my best friend of my scholarly findings. I was permitted that day to walk—with great care—across the table to the centre of one of the false giants' garments and smooth it with my hands. In my stock-inged feet, I stepped over the weft and warp of fabric, its give and softness and promise awakening my toes to its gentle bulk and beauty. I remember the sound of thunking metal punching the morning air, just as I hear it now.

Now. She calls for tea from the kitchen next door. Servants replace their cooling irons and sit on low stools along the walls.

'Why, Teacher-Servant. There you stood—a young boy in the ironing room of the City of Servants, making a nuisance of yourself, your arms full of dictionaries. What were we to do with you?' She winks at me over her teacup. 'It is not so many years ago, young man, that you found yourself trapped inside the yards of cotton in which you'd entangled your legs while trying to be of *assistance.* It took us a few moments to extract you, as you kicked against the red dress, bringing it to most humorous life. We'd have rescued you sooner, but we were caught in bouts of laughter at your predicament.'

I remember. I love Senior Iron-Servant as I love my own mother, and even though I have thirty years and some months, I am a child when she teases me.

'Dear Senior Iron-Servant! You make a fool of me!'

'Oh, blame nature for that, lad. Not me.'

It is a familiar and beloved exchange. I do not find fault in her gentle mocking. Just this morning, a Wrist-Servant tumbled to the hard ground while moving one of Nuala's great arms so that the Clothing-Servants could dry her wooden hands after her shower. The Wrist-Servants are lean and fit, but we are all out of practice. The false giants we trained upon did not fully prepare us for our work with a living, breathing Giant. We do not mock the Servant's misfortune. We are only relieved that he was not hurt, save for his pride.

We finish our tea, and the Iron-Servants return to their task. Three Servants stand at the end of the table holding the open neck of the dress, four more at its bottom opening. They flip it, changing places as they turn the yards of cotton, tug the edges to pull the dress straight and crisp. The cool irons are traded for hot, and the sweet scent of fragrant fabric stings the air. Pressing and smoothing for Nuala's new day.

Rhythmic swish and slide and thunk of metal on cotton on wood take the Servants into their own thoughts, and at these times, Senior Iron-Servant gives them a story.

'I am silvered now,' she begins, 'but I was once as young and strong as you are now, though I was not nearly as striking.'

'You flatter me!' I am thrilled by her attention, even though her words have not varied in years.

'He who expects flattery will hear it in every word uttered near him,' she says, her iron slapping the morning air alive with the birds of the earliest hours.

I become serious and sit near her, and the other Iron-Servants slow their work and place their irons more gently to better hear her words. In the City of Servants, I always came early in the morning to listen to her stories, and this one is sad but familiar.

'I once had a small, golden-haired girl of my own, so long gone now. So long dead. I would stand at my ironing board before she awoke. Iron the dress she would wear to school that day. We were not wealthy, but the child's dress would always be pressed and ready to meet the day. How does one replace a lost daughter?'

Some answer as they always do: 'One does not.'

'My little girl resembled Nuala in that they both have such clear, searching eyes. Though my girl could laugh and play on her own, Nuala's curiosity matches hers. What little I've seen of it.

'Teacher-Servant, I can think of no one more suited to this important task than you. No one who could better teach our Nuala all that she needs to know, all that she must learn to live among us. And most important, to help us understand how best to serve her. To find out why she has awoken. Why now, and why for us.'

'Thank you, Senior Iron-Servant, for these kind words.' I stand and embrace the best friend I have. 'I will not trouble you and your staff any longer. As you know, I can be clumsy, and if I stay, I am liable to get myself tangled in this pretty red dress!'

Small chuckles rise up and twirl in the wooden blades of the ceiling fans.

'I take my leave of you all. My duties await me, although until I know Nuala's mind, I will not know of what they consist. I bid you good morning, and may your joys be trebled in the Service.'

'And yours as well, Teacher-Servant,' they say in unison.

Senior Iron-Servant's wrists are lean and ready. Her greying curls tucked behind her ears, she swings the sadiron over the cloth, sometimes setting it aside to smooth the fabric with her fingers. Some wrinkles must be treated by hand.

The

Clothing-Servants carry the heavy garment to where Nuala stands in her showering place. They fan out the crimson dress and pass it up to those standing on ladders. Those above fit the dress over Nuala's head. Slip her wrists through the holes in the great sheet of fabric, and do up each button, down to the gap that is open to allow the long fingers of the Engine to enter her back. Her Walking-Servants lift her legs and her Clothing-Servants fit her with white socks and black shoes. I needn't supervise the dressing of Nuala, but she needs me near.

'Nuala, do you like your pretty dress?'

'Teacher-Servant, it is beautiful. I am loved, am I not?'

'You are.'

We will not let her be rumpled. Nothing will be out of place when our Puppet Queen first walks her city, when her citizens see her full height for the first time.

I change into my soft slippers and Head-Servant sends the rope ladder down to my waiting hands. I climb to Nuala's shoulder, roll up the ladder and lay the coil beside me next to her left earlobe. For the first time, we walk together. She is too overwhelmed to speak to me yet. To talk of the wonders she sees before her, above her, and below her. Now, she is content to walk and to let her Servants guide us to the fountain at the city centre. I ask the Servants to bend her at the waist so that she may see herself for the first time reflected in the great pool of water.

'Who is this, Teacher-Servant? Who is this Giant?'

'Little one. That is yourself you see in the water. And do you see the small man standing upon you? That is your shoulder, and upon it is your Teacher-Servant. I am six feet tall, but compared to your great height, I look a tiny creature, do I not? There are not two of me. The one you see in the water is false, and yet it is true, because it is me. The Giant you see is false, and yet it is you.' I grasp the metal handle fitted to Nuala's throat for me and use it to steady myself as her Servants lift her upright.

Nuala sees the citizens standing on the far side of the fountain, their reflections doubling them, an upside-down parade of themselves. The people stand and yet they ripple on the water: waving, laughing, weeping. Finally, a Giant has come!

I tell her, 'Beloved, those are the small people, the people the size of me. They are citizens who are not lucky enough to serve you. But they may stand near the fountains of the city and watch you. Did you see yourself mirrored in the water?

It is the same with the citizens. In water, we see ourselves twinned; we see the rippling echoes of ourselves. We are all two, Nuala. That which we know ourselves to be, and that which we show. That which is reflected in the water.'

'Teacher-Servant, why do the small people of the city watch me as they do? Why do they cry and call to me? Have they never seen a Giant before?' Her gaze is a gift to the people she sees mirrored in the water. They wave and weep in response. This gaze is not the gift of the first gaze, but I am the only one who will feel that in our lifetime.

'No, they have not, my Nuala. You are the first they've seen.'

'But are there other Giants? Where are they, Teacher-Servant? When will I see them?'

'Here there is only you, little one. But oh, the stories I will tell you of Giants in other lands! When I tell you stories of the Land of Giants, your heart will fill, love will surge in and take you over, make your every oaken nerve sing with desire to see them. How you will wish to travel there with me. How you will wish to travel with me to the Land of Giants on a great ship: a vessel that sails on water.'

'This is too much, Teacher-Servant. I have learned *water*, but I cannot understand *ship*.'

'Look far, far ahead of you, beyond the granite buildings you see in the distance. Beyond that, you may see the foggy outlines of the great sea. On it, the ships dance on the waters. Ships larger even than you. A riding, a bumping, a misting of salty water will rock you into a deep sleep, and when you awaken, the Land of Giants will be before you, the arms of the Giants the length of this street we now traverse. Their eyes only on you.'

'I see the water, Teacher-Servant, but I do not see the ships you speak of. Perhaps my eyes are not made for such seeing.'

'These marvels are far away, Nuala, and far in the time beyond ours. For now, be content with our walking and seeing in this radiant city, and with the love I already bear you. You, only a few days old, and on your first walk.'

Her thoughts are full of what she thinks waves must be, their rolling. Inside, she tumbles and sinks with the movement of what she imagines the water must do, and through the thrashings, I am with her in her mind, atop her shoulder, my tiny weight upon her shoulder, loving her from beside her exquisite face.

Next to her left cheek, I watch the Walking-Servants look up as they lift and lower her great wooden legs. Three Servants lift each leg, jumping to pull the great ropes, and handing them off to the next in line to keep her moving, moving. The wind over the tall buildings stirs her hair, whistling through the spaces in her throat and kneecaps as they bend and give.

'Why must I see through these...what do you call them?'

'Wires, my child.'

'Wires. Everything I see is through these wires. I cannot look at the buildings, the small people of the city, or my Servants without seeing them. You may see the world as a clear place, as may my other Servants. There are no wires in front of your faces. Why am I not permitted?'

'My child, in the Land of Giants, there are no wires. No clips or ropes. No Engines. The Giants there may move any way they like.'

'Oh, Teacher-Servant. When may we go?'

'Patience. You have only just awoken here. You must learn *here*. My Nuala, I know you are full with questions and each is important, but I am only one Servant and cannot spend the length of each day answering them. Practice looking and listening, for these are skills you will need as you grow and learn. Watch and learn the ways your Servants help you stride through your city. Yes, you see through wires, but the people working those wires love you. They love you above their families. Above their own lives. Do you understand?'

'Teacher-Servant, I have learned that moving my legs is difficult work. My Servants' faces are shining up toward me, but I see that they have to run to try to keep up with my legs, which are so much larger and longer than theirs. When we find the Land of Giants, Teacher-Servant, will I still see small people there? And will they love me?'

'I do not want you to find the Land of Giants, my beloved. For then you would want to leave me to be with others of your kind.'

'I will do as you instruct, Teacher-Servant.'

'Now hush, and look. Look, my child. See the tiny city through your Giant eyes. These are birds that fly around you, curious to know what you are. They may light on your shoulders as you walk, but do not fear them. They own the skies and the air above the buildings. They want only to see who commands the heights over which they usually hold dominion.'

The Servants below bend and pull the great ropes that move my Nuala's legs and arms. They, so pleased to be working for a Puppet Queen, no strain shows on their faces.

'Now see below.' I look to the chair hanging behind Nuala's skull and signal Head-Servant to turn her face downward. 'You may see the children at your feet. Watch them running between your legs and listen to them calling up to you. Do you hear how they sing your name to you? *Nuuuuuuu-laaaa.* They love you as well. They are you, but smaller. For you yourself are a child.'

After a moment, Head-Servant lifts her head to look out at the land before her. The buildings and grime and beauty of her city.

'Little one, do you remember the way you looked at me when first you saw me at your bedside?' I reach for a few stray strands of hair the wind has blown into the coiled metal of her throat, and pull them behind her ear, kissing the lobe as I do so.

'Yes, Teacher-Servant. I had only just awoken, and yet I knew all that I needed to know about you.'

'You gave me the gift of your first gaze,' I tell her. 'When your Servants do something kind for you, the only reward they desire is your gaze. Do not forget this, my Nuala.'

I signal again to Head-Servant. 'Now, look down! Look at the people walking with bags of food to eat, vessels holding sweet wine to drink. See their faces turned upward in wonder. They have heard the stories, but now you are among them. They can scarcely believe you are here.'

A citizen in a hurry drops a bottle of wine. It shatters on the stones, wine and splinters of glass shooting across Nuala's feet.

'What has happened, Teacher-Servant?'

'It is nothing, my love. Sometimes the city people are clumsy and drop things. When they fall and shatter as that bottle did, we say the fallen thing is broken.' A shop owner offers a broom, and we stop to allow a Walking-Servant to brush the deep crimson liquid and brown shards from Nuala's shoes.

'Do you see the people walking as we are doing now, running, riding bicycles between your feet? The people below you with armloads of wood for the autumn fire you see burning in the square, wrapped and fragrant bouquets of white and yellow flowers with velvet petals and swaying leaves. Look how each one stops to wave up at you, to call your name, to strew leaves upon the ground where you walk.

'See how your citizens hold long loaves of bread, or books, or their children, or pieces of machinery. Now look up. Over the tops of the buildings, birds roosting under the eaves, then nests and birdlings on the roofs. The everything of it all! All awash in grandness and height and sheets of metal and iron and stone and glass, the tops of the streetlamps down and down below.

'Remember this. Remember what you see and what you feel, and remember me here. For this is my weight upon your shoulder. This is the weight of the steps I take when I am astride you, nesting upon you, where I will always be, my Nuala.'

Though

they are old and have not been worn in anyone's memory, Senior Iron-Servant has pulled the purple hat and raincoat from the giant wooden trunk in Nuala's sleeping quarters. The garments are musty from disuse and are too big for Nuala, but my friend has given them a thorough airing, a quick tailoring. Freshened them with lavender oil and wind. This morning, I fingered the weight of them as they hung on the line, the threat of clouds thick in the moist air.

Nuala and I have been walking for several weeks, and each day but today, the sun shone as if for her alone. I have feared falling asleep on her shoulder as we stride through the city, the lull of new summer warmth on my face, the heat of her wooden cheek against the cool skin of my own.

'I wish it were raining and then not raining and then raining again, Teacher-Servant,' she thinks to me as I hang from the Engine's rope ladder, suspended before her throat, unbuttoning her raincoat. My fingers are clumsy on the giant circles, their size making me feel my hands are not my own. I have been in the rain for hours, answering Nuala's questions over and over, and now these buttons.

'Why wish such a thing, little one?'

'Because your hands would always be here, near my face, as it is you who buttons and unbuttons me when the rain stops and starts. I am pleased with the new purple coat and hat I am permitted to wear, Teacher-Servant. But I know that you and Head-Servant must help me to take them off. I know that when the Engine gives me a shower, then that is the correct time to have water flowing over my body. Before I have my socks and shoes on and my pretty red dress.'

'What else do you know, Nuala?'

'I know your cool hands on my throat, Teacher-Servant.'

I snatch my fingers from the button with which I'm struggling.

'No, Teacher-Servant. Do not take your hands from me. I do not mind their chill, for even though they are cold, your care warms me. I want your hands upon me. I know Head-Servant is behind me now, helping you take off my rain hat. But it is your hands I want. Your hands that push the cap off my head, yours that smooth my hair and place it behind my ears. There are no hands but yours. Yours inside my hair, and against my face.'

I work my way along the ropes, and reach to fix the little braid I made for her yesterday when we walked the city. I sat on her left shoulder and fastened it with a ribbon I found in a long-ago box my mother gave me in the City of Servants, and put in my pocket on impulse. As I played with Nuala's hair, I found myself shaping her a braid.

'Teacher-Servant?' I swing back before her face. 'I can see the shape of you. I can see the green in your eyes, and I can see your long curls. I feel your hands brushing my lips. Do you see how well I have learned all that you have taught me about our parts? About how we work together?'

'I am pleased with your education, Nuala.' My tasks complete, the raincoat and hat removed, her hair tidied, I have no reason to stay on this ladder before her. I lean my body into her face and stretch across the expanse of her cheek to see that the nails holding her mouth closed are secure and not in need of oil, even though I know they are not.

I feel a wooden kiss of such ardour that I am pulled toward it. My lips part against cool wood at the edge of her ever-closed mouth, and my pelvis drops. I break with love, with yearning so sudden, so violent I cannot move. Cannot read her. Cannot speak.

She is quiet in her mind, but her wooden skin is heated. Her eyes bore into me. Her child-mind whispers me, 'Is this what Giant love feels like, Teacher-Servant?'

'Oh, my little one. The only Giant love I know is that which I feel from you. I do not know any other Giants. Perhaps one day you will know a Giant's kiss, a Giant's hands in your hair. But for now, you are mine and I am yours, and my tiny hands will have to be enough. Though they are small, they are made for no work but this. To serve and to soothe you.'

I climb up to the Engine's long, curved arms over Nuala's head. I am shaken. Unsteady.

Tonight

I draw trees. A dozen for her. The trees of her body. I tint the leaves with green chalk. Set them around her room so that she may feel forest.

Through

the windows we watch on our walks, Nuala sees tiny flickers inside the homes of the city people. 'Candles,' I answer. 'They are little warming fires that also give light and allow the small people to read books.'

'Tell me about books and light and fire, Teacher-Servant. I saw many fires under the sky when we first walked through the parks of the city, and many people holding out their hands to them, but why do the city people love them so?'

It is bedtime, and bedtime is the time for stories. For days, Nuala has wanted to hear of the Land of Giants. What I tell her is from imagination and not knowledge. It is a welcome change to talk of other things: things that she can feel and see.

'Tell me of fire, Teacher-Servant.'

'The small people make fires when they want to feel warm. When they want to see one another in soft light, and when they want to talk of important events in their lives. Though they have other means by which to bring light and warmth into their homes, some prefer candles as they help people feel closer to one another.

'Candles are made of wax, but fires are made of wood and when the wood burns, the warmth brings the small people together to talk and sing and drink the wine you saw some of them carrying. This is what fires are for. For love and friendliness and warmth.

'But you must be wary of fire, my love. Just as it can burn people if they approach unwisely, it can also hurt you because of that of which you are made.' I lie beside her left ear, the length of me on her great pillow. Why at bedtime? My every instinct tells me I should hold back the story of fire, and although I am fatigued and weary of her questions today, my work is clear: I must tell Nuala all she wants to know, save the Two Great Secrets.

'Of what am I made? And why may I not speak?' she asks. 'Why do I have a mouth if I cannot open it to give voice to my thoughts the way you and my other Servants may do? Why may I speak only to you?'

'One answer at a time, beloved. I am your Teacher-Servant, and speaking to you is a gift given only to me. So it is now and so it has ever been, in anyone's memory. It is possible that the mouths of the Giants once opened, but no Giant who has ever awoken has the power of speech. Your mouth is fixed shut with nails that no one dare tamper with.'

'Could you not tamper with these...*nails*, Teacher-Servant? How I yearn to speak. What does my voice sound like? I would never stop speaking, I have so much to say.'

'Perhaps that is why you cannot speak, my child. You would never stop! No one else could ever speak again, for you would always be talking, my little chatterbox. Your Giant voice would carry across the city and it would be all anyone could hear!'

'How you do tease me, Teacher-Servant! Then tell me of what I am made.' I lift my body to stand next to her, climb the small ladder against her face, place my elbows on her cheek, and chin my face in my palms. I look into the burnt emerald depths of her left eye.

'I know that I am not made of you,' she says. 'Nor am I made of that which makes my other Servants, or the people of the city. Your hands are warm and you may move as you wish without wires. I may not. Of what am I made?'

'You are made of metal and wood, my child.'

Her thoughts burst into the colour of fear. 'I am what they burn in their fires!' Her cheek against my thigh tingles with her anxiety, and I must be the one to dissipate it. I do not always know if I am equipped for this work, this questioning, her every emotion drilling into me.

'I will never let that happen, little one.' I stroke her cheek. 'We Servants are made of flesh and blood. What you are made of is stronger than that which forms your Servants. You are built upon a sturdy framework, my child. Do you remember the picture of the tallest tree I drew for you to look at? Imagine that great tree, that formidable and grounded tree inside of you. A tree that stretches from the earth, up through your back...'

'Where the Engine's long arm reaches?'

'Yes, that is right.' I feel her great desire to close her eyes, but she is unhooked and Seeing-Servant is long asleep. I do it for her. First her left eye, and then I walk on her pillow with my ladder, around the top of her head to the right side of her face. I climb onto her cheek and lay my body against her to pull the veneer down over the great eye. I wish her mind could quiet itself as easily. I curl into the hollow at the side of her nose.

'The tree inside you grows up, up, and up, my love. Up into your shoulders, into your neck. The great tree reaches into your head. Its thick branches spread out into your mind. Its leaves are your thoughts.' I move down her face to stroke her lips to still the wild thought-leaves now that she cannot see me.

'The thought-leaves sway and rustle in your mind, and they smell of sweet summer. It is that which supports you, Nuala. Not the Engine's fist of steel, or your Servants pulling on the cables attached to your kneecaps and wrists. You are built around an oak of unparalleled strength, an oak as old as this city is old. Nothing can topple you, Nuala. Your thoughts are forever-thoughts. The great tree inside you is ageless and immortal.'

'When may I see this tree, Teacher-Servant?'

'How tiresome you are this evening! Tomorrow, you shall see many trees like the one inside you, my beloved, if you are quiet now and go to sleep.'

Her voice is distant and languid. 'Who made me, Teacher-Servant?'

I wait until I'm certain she is on the cusp of sleep. 'I cannot tell you, my tall and lovely oak. It is enough for now that you are cherished and that you cherish in return. Now sleep. Sleep and dream.'

She woke with intellect, with language, with the curiosity of a girl who'd been awake for a decade. And all of it inside my head, overpowering me with intensity and thrusting.

'When will we see the trees, Teacher-Servant?'

The persistent question rattles my nerve endings. 'Little one, I told you not a moment ago that when I see the trees, I will point them out to you. You shall not miss them.'

'But I want so to meet them, Teacher-Servant. I want to hear their stories!'

I stifle unkind thoughts of nails stopping up her voice in my head. 'Remember that the trees might not speak to you,' I say. 'I cannot know for certain. Yes, you are all creatures of wood, but you must be prepared. You may not be able to speak to the trees any more than you can speak with the wooden trim around the window of your bedroom. For both are made of wood.'

'But the trim around my window is not Giant, Teacher-Servant.'

Her logic amuses me, despite the monotony of her questioning, and I laugh as we round the last corner on our way to the cemetery at the edge of the city. I signal to Seeing-Servant to move her eyes to the swaying treetops. 'There they are, my love. Oak and spruce and yellowwood and pine—all tall and lovely as you.'

'Why do they not walk to meet me, Teacher-Servant? How I want to hold them!'

'You may do so, little one. Remember, I told you that trees are rooted to the ground. It is that which holds them strong and tall, just as the Engine and your Servants help hold *you* strong and tall. It is the wind that stirs their leaves to life. It is the same wind that moves your hair on either side of your face.'

We walk toward the tallest and nearest tree, an early-summer, moss-covered pine, its torso weaving under the sky, creaking and swaying.

'Would you like to embrace this tree, Nuala?'

'Teacher-Servant, but for the touch of your flesh-and-blood hands, I have never wanted anything more.'

We move Nuala, slowly and with great care, to the heft of the trunk. The Wrist-Servants swish through centuries of spongy needles to lift her great arms into the air so that she may feel the knotty surface against her face, the insides of her elbows.

Her yearning washes me. A pull greater than that toward me. This, for one of her own kind: a tall and steady tree in love with its motion, its resilience and beauty. It needs nothing, no one, but the earth below and the sun and rain above. Its far-above canopy rains needles down on my Nuala and me as she whispers and coos to the tree in her arms.

'I do not have a *family*,' she says, 'but Teacher-Servant has helped me to understand what the word means. You are my family now.'

'**Oh,** Teacher-Servant, the things the tree told me! It said I was the prettiest Giant it had ever seen! It told me of other Giants who had embraced it, but said that my embrace was much sweeter than theirs.'

'Little one, it is now *you* who are fabricating stories.'

'The tree did not tell me in words, Teacher-Servant, but in the pull of its body. The way it leaned toward me when my Wrist-Servants helped me to embrace it. I knew it was speaking the truth.'

I pull needles from her hair. 'Such a mess you are, my love!' I brush them from her shoulder, and I burn to ask her what I am, if not her family.

An open window on the sixth floor. A block of flats in a
street we have not yet visited in our weeks of walking and of
Nuala's learning. A balcony with wooden shuttered doors open
to the street and to the city, and on the balcony, a wooden table
and two chairs, each with a ruffled sun-bleached cushion upon
it, and sheer white curtains flirting with the chairs, draping
themselves over the backs, the cool air singing through the flat
within. As we approach, the beloved tree fades from Nuala's
mind, as quickly as it came. So much a child, my tall and lovely
Queen.

'Oh, Teacher-Servant! May we look inside? I think this must
be the prettiest place I have ever seen!' The building is stone,
and is chipped in places along the edges of balconies. I signal
the Servants to stop, and I call to the young woman I see sitting
in the blue-painted kitchen inside the old flat.

'Good morning! My name is Teacher-Servant, and I am
Nuala's guardian. Nuala would like to look inside your home
through this open door. Would you agree to that?'

'Of course.' She approaches, her flowery dress dancing
around her legs in the breeze. She wraps her thick pink cardigan
around her body. 'It's fortunate that you've arrived on my free
day from the sewing workshop. Mother and I like to spend
this day together each week.'

An older woman turns to us, nods her head and blows
Nuala a kiss.

'Word of Nuala's awakening has spread throughout the
city, Teacher-Servant,' the young woman says. 'Those of us not

in the Service were delighted by rumours that she might be walking our streets.'

A few stray needles drop to the balcony. 'Ah, I see you have been to the forest,' she says, picking up the delicate spines and placing them on the table. 'Please, allow the child to look as she wishes. My mother and I will continue our game while she satisfies her curiosity.'

The young woman turns back to the table where, it becomes apparent, the two are drinking tea from china cups and playing a game in which they take turns reaching into a purple velvet bag and extracting wooden tiles with the letters of our alphabet inscribed on them. The board is marked with squares in many colours. I can see several with instructions painted on them, but I cannot read the words from this distance.

'This is not like the room where I sleep, Teacher-Servant.' Nuala's excitement is rising, her frame bent to allow her to see inside the flat. To one side, a tidy kitchen, to the other, a neatly made single bed.

'I am a Giant, so my room is very large, but this room is small because the women at the table are small. What is this *game* the young woman talks of, Teacher-Servant?'

'I do not know, little one. Excuse me, Miss. Nuala is curious about the game you are playing. I have never seen one like it.'

'It's a word game, Teacher-Servant. My mother and I take turns choosing letters from this bag. We form words upon the board and tell stories according to the instructions on the squares we choose. The words don't have to exist in our language. We often make them up. Usually, we follow no rules and we rarely keep score. There are only letters and stories.

'I have chosen a square that reads *Tell of the Past*. Mother, here is my story for you. In the time before our memory, a

Great Giant walked our city. She felt at home with the small people, but it was the trees for which she yearned.'

'I have heard this story before, my darling,' Mother says, 'but perhaps Nuala would like to hear it.'

Nuala's brain is a mass of molten desire for story. 'I can assure you she would,' I say, bowing to the older woman.

'A *word* game about the past and stories! Oh, Teacher-Servant! How beautiful these women are! They are not made of sturdy oaks, but they look as strong as the tree of which I am made. What is the brown liquid they drink? Why does it make them close their eyes? That liquid is the colour of the wood of my hands! Why do they...?'

'Little one. You are becoming quite a nuisance. Allow the young woman to tell her story for you.'

She walks out onto the balcony, holding her cup of tea. She places the drink on the small table and tucks her legs under her in one of the chairs.

'In a time before ours,' she begins, as though reciting from a storybook her mother had read to her when she was a girl, 'a lovely Giant walked the city. Only the oldest of citizens remember her now, and they remember her as a sketchy picture from their youth. The last Giant to walk our city walked long before I was born, before your Teacher-Servant was born, even before Mother was born.

'The books say that she was two hundred feet tall, that her hair was long and flowing black, so thick that birds were often startled when they became tangled in it.'

I have taken a comfortable position sitting cross-legged, but I stand, grip the handle at Nuala's neck, and reach out to receive the cup of tea the old woman holds out to me. I sit down again and sip. The tea is strong and sweet, rosehips and spice.

'The Giant lay sleeping for centuries in the City of Servants, as all Giants do, until she awoke and gave the gift of her first gaze to the only Teacher-Servant in our memory. The Servants were ready, and learned by reading the ancient texts how to operate the Great Giant. They called her the Puppet Queen and she ruled benevolently for many years. They say it is because of this Giant that we no longer have violence or crime in our city. She abolished money, made all citizens and Servants equal in her eyes, and allowed us only to barter with our goods.'

'Where is she now, Teacher-Servant? Why may I not see her and speak to her?'

'Forgive me, Miss. We must not interrupt when someone is telling a story, Nuala. I shan't tell you again.' I lean toward the lovely young woman, curled in her chair. 'Please go on.'

The old woman brings the teapot out to the balcony and refreshes her daughter's cup. She places a book on the table, lays a withered hand on her daughter's head, and sits next to her. I look into my cup, my sudden longing for the touch of my own mother's hand making me shake.

'It's quite all right, Teacher-Servant. I know the curiosity of children. It is hard to tame, but so easy to cherish. Was Nuala asking about this Giant?'

'You are insightful, Miss. She was indeed.' The older woman picks up the picture book, which she holds up for Nuala to see. *Tales of Our Great Giants.* She opens it to a picture of a Mother-Giant, and holds it as close to Nuala's eyes as her infirm arms will allow.

'Nuala,' the young woman continues, 'no one knows what happened to the Great Giant. One morning, the Waking-Servants and her Teacher-Servant overslept and were late for work. When they arrived at the sleeping room—the room you sleep in now but with a much larger bed—the Giant was gone, to their great alarm. Walls had been knocked down, and the trail of her movement could be seen through the city. It was as though a child had walked through a shop filled with delicate teacups balanced on tilting shelves, with no adult to hold her hand.

'Bits of brick and concrete were all over the streets. The citizens and the Servants followed the path of broken things to the edge of town, where they lost the trail. At the tree line, the Giant vanished. Tales are told of a great ship, large enough to transport her across the water to the Land of Giants.

'Without the daily showers and the oiling of the Giant's great wrists and kneecaps, it is not clear how she took care of herself, but it seems, her purpose here accomplished, that she did, for she was never seen again. The people had relied on her for everything. And then she was gone. A silence and a longing settled over the land as the people of the Great City struggled to find meaning on their own. For when the leader is gone, if the people have not learned to lead themselves, the leader has served no purpose.'

Nuala has gone quiet. The moment hangs.

'Oh, dear. Maybe I've said too much,' the young woman whispers, holding her hand to her pretty lips.

'Please do not fear,' I assure her, stretching to hand her my empty teacup. 'These stories are part of Nuala's story, and she will hear them all in time. I thank you for your generosity. We will leave you now to return to your game.'

I turn to Nuala, to pull her back from wherever she has gone. 'Nuala, my love, have you remembered to give the women the gift of your gaze for allowing you to look inside their home, and to thank them for the story?'

I signal to Seeing-Servant to turn her eyes toward the young woman. The women rise and return Nuala's gaze.

'Come any time, child,' the young woman says. Her mother gives a small wave.

When the gift is given, Head-Servant turns the great face from the window. Nuala's energy thunders with desire. From deep inside, she thinks me a low groan.

'Now now, my child. We can return another time. The small people do not always like to have Giants peering through their windows. Imagine if there were people always looking in at *your* room.'

'There are always small people looking at me, Teacher-Servant. You know this as well as I do. I want to be small. I want to be in the room with the young woman and the word game. Have you not told me I am in command here, Teacher-Servant?'

'You are, little one. But calm your thoughts. They are driving me quite mad. Until you understand your Servants, your city, and the small people you see, you are still a student.'

'I wish to learn nothing but more stories of the Great Giant who walked before me.'

As we move through the days and weeks, Nuala and I return again and again to the block of flats that houses the young woman. We stand at her window the same time each week: the day on which the young woman does not work in the sewing workshop, and is free to play the word game with her mother, and visit with Nuala and me. We arrive just as the young woman reaches for the game in the high cupboard above the sink. The kettle is whistling on the stovetop. Each time, the two women are patient and kind with us as Nuala's great eyes scan the room she's come to know as well as she knows the weight of me on her shoulder, my touch on her eyelids.

'Teacher-Servant! They are playing the game again today!' Each visit, it is as though she is seeing the word game for the first time, so excited is she by it and by the words the women spell, even though she cannot understand them. At my command, the Engine bends Nuala further at the waist. The older woman hands me a cup of tea.

Nuala's mind is a mass of mismatched parts, gears grating as they spark against one another. She has no mechanism to stop it. So active are her thoughts that I find myself exhausted, almost wishing for the emptiness of the minds of those Giants who did not come to life when I was a young man learning to wipe their faces clean.

'Teacher-Servant, I love this small house. I love these women. I want to...'

'Now, Nuala,' I say to her aloud. 'I am in conversation with these women who are being very kind to us today. You must wait your turn to say what you need to say.'

She thinks me a quiet yes.

'What is Nuala saying today, Teacher-Servant?' the tall young woman asks from her position on one of the balcony chairs. Her forearms glow healthy and tanned in the mid-morning sun, an orange pullover draped across her shoulders, the sleeves tied over her chest. 'Everyone is so curious as to what she thinks, but can anyone be as curious as me? After all, she comes to my window every week. One would think she might get tired of watching Mother and I playing the word game and drinking tea.'

'One would think! As it happens, at the moment she is telling me how deeply she loves your home, how she loves to watch you and your mother play the word game. How she loves your stories, and how deeply she loves you.'

'I am honoured that she loves me, Teacher-Servant. I have a growing fondness for her too. Of course, I have no claim on this little one, and cannot hear her thoughts, so I must trust that you tell me the truth.' Her eyebrow lifts in a moment of mockery. 'Maybe you're making up Nuala's thoughts in order to flatter me.'

'I assure you, Miss, that what I speak is the truth: that the strength of Nuala's love for you occasionally overwhelms me. Why, sometimes it makes me jealous!'

We laugh together and I hold out my empty cup and thank her for the tea. Her long, strong hands reach up to mine.

'We have taken too much of your time today, ladies,' I say, signalling to Seeing-Servant to move Nuala's eyes from the blue room. While Nuala's mind is engaged in the movement,

I bend low and ask in a quiet voice, 'I would very much like to have a drink with you. Would this please you, Miss?'

'I'd like that,' she says.

'Do you know the alehouse at the centre of town? The one the Servants frequent?'

'I do. I shall meet you there the day after tomorrow when Nuala takes her nap. I have an afternoon free that day.'

The Engine forces Nuala to stand upright, and the Wrist- and Walking-Servants prepare to move her away at my command. She is strong-willed, my child. If she had her own way, we would stand looking into this small home day and night.

'Oh, but you tell me she is beautiful, my dear friend. You tell me with your eyes and hands, if not with your words. I understand Nuala's fascination with her because I see her through your eyes.'

Senior Iron-Servant pours me more thick ale from the pottery jug. 'She is clearly a compelling storyteller, and has woven you into her stories as surely as Nuala has been caught up. It seems that not only Nuala is fascinated,' she says. She leans across the tavern table and pats my cheek as though I were the little boy I once was, one infatuated with a girl to whom I was too shy to speak.

I permit no one else to tease me about my motives or thoughts where Nuala is concerned, but as she is so fond of reminding me, Senior Iron-Servant remembers when I was a tiny lad, looking up at false giants, longing for the honour to work with them. She remembers combing my long hair, pulling me into her embrace when I said goodbye to my mother forever, when we left the City of Servants to serve Nuala. She has earned the right to say what she likes.

'I am meeting her here in two days' time. That shall either set tongues wagging, or still them for good. I hope for the latter, but expect the former.'

Two Kitchen-Servants walk into the tavern and nod at us. 'Teacher-Servant. Senior Iron-Servant,' one calls, tipping his hat to my friend. 'May your joy be trebled in the Service.'

'And yours as well,' we say as we raise our glasses to them. The tavern is busy today and I prefer this din to quiet. In the noise and tumult of laughing, drinking Servants and citizens, it is far easier for me to shield my thoughts from Nuala, but more importantly, I am able to close out her never-ending desire for word games, all scrambled with her yearning for a poised young woman with long hair and bright eyes.

I turn back to Senior Iron-Servant. 'I fear the other Servants think my motives suspect, my friend. Each day I hear someone whispering that it is for *myself* that we return and return to the same rooms each week. It is not! I swear by this hand that it is Nuala's desire.'

'You needn't convince *me*,' she says. 'Teacher-Servant, you needn't convince anyone. Why shouldn't you have a drink with a lovely young woman who is not a Servant? You are as entitled to happiness as any of us.

'As to the Servants' resentment, each person in this tavern knows that if you were not the right one for the important position you hold, Nuala would have given some other Servant the gift of her first gaze. You knew when you applied for the job that with it would come jealousy, misunderstandings, whisperings.'

'True, my wise friend. But it makes me no less lonely. Just yesterday, I heard two Wrist-Servants talking when they did not know I was near. One said to the other, *a life of leisure for that one. He does nothing but ride her shoulder and tell her pretty stories. We're just as deserving of knowing Nuala's feelings and thoughts, but I swear he's keeping them to himself and lording it over us.*'

'Again, a professional hazard you knew you would face,' she says, and waves at the tavern owner for more ale. I am slightly off balance, and worry I shall not be able to shut out Nuala's dreams tonight. On the other hand, a head full of ale might be just what I need to do that.

'I fear the job will become more tedious than it already is. When we are not visiting the young woman and her mother, we walk other streets. I try to interest her in other houses, other pleasures, but to no avail. What goes through her mind never varies: word games, trees, tea. Truly, if my colleagues had the first idea how head-splittingly repetitive her thoughts and dreams are, her desire to do the same things day after day, they would not trade places with me for the world. But even if I tried to explain to them, I doubt they would understand. She has no control over the way her mind crowds mine, but as she learns, it becomes more powerful. Sometimes violent, and always with all a child's ruthless desiring.'

'And yet she shares it all with you. Are you able to keep thoughts of your past from her?'

'So far, yes. I see no point in telling her of my life before her. It's best I not think of that long-ago place, as I do not need the added burden. If Nuala is capable of jealousy, I have no doubt it will be as violent as any of her other emotions.

'But I cannot imagine it will be much longer until she has access to my memories, good or ill. It is only here that I'm able to separate our minds fully.'

I drain my mug and pour myself another. I do not work again until Nuala's bedtime. I shall be sober by then.

She yearns to speak, to force the bitter nails from her mouth. Perhaps it once opened. Now is it closed forever. Her desire to talk to the young woman is so overpowering it haunts my nights and fills my days, peering through windows into rooms she may never enter.

I rise when the young woman enters the tavern. She wears blue summer trousers and a white blouse. If my fellow Servants notice her, I do not see. She is all I see.

'Good afternoon,' I say as I pull out a chair for her across from mine. 'I cannot tell you how pleased I am that you chose to spend part of your free day with me.' I signal to the bartender for a jug of ale and two glasses.

'I was delighted that you asked me, Teacher-Servant. We've not had a chance to speak without Nuala hearing. Does she hear us now?'

'I am teaching myself not to hear her, and to hide my thoughts from her. Occasionally, a song running through my head will be enough, but if she is passionate—as she always is with her thoughts of you—it takes more than a simple song to banish them. I find the atmosphere here at the alehouse most conducive to having free time in my mind. The blend of voices stills my thoughts, and she hears the same hubbub I do.'

She pours ale into our glasses and we touch them together. She gives the toast. 'To Nuala.'

'If we must,' I say and take a long drink.

'I'm curious, Teacher-Servant. How is your life different from those not in Service? I see that your job entails the education and supervision of Nuala, but you say that you must close yourself off from her thoughts. Do her thoughts no longer give you pleasure?'

'Where to begin? Nuala's education is indeed my domain, but she learns at such an exponential rate, that sometimes, it feels as if my brain is tearing itself from my skull. All her thoughts enter me: everything she thinks and feels, and most invasively, everything she dreams. I do not fault her for this last, for she has no control over what enters her mind when she sleeps. For the rest, I truly feel that the bulk of my job consists of reining in her thoughts. There is no time for any sort of education in the traditional sense.'

'Then how do the other Servants' jobs differ from my own? I work each day in the sewing workshop, sewing buttons on the lapels of the Servants' uniforms, among other tasks. It's likely I finished the lapel on the very uniform you wear right now.'

'For you, and for the other citizens who are not Servants, there is purpose. Even if your tasks seem inconsequential, they are not. For look at how neat my lapels are! You and your colleagues are to be thanked for that.

'Your work has meaning, and tangible results. You may see your labour, and you may be proud of it. I have no such meaning in my life. I left the City of Servants to become Nuala's Teacher-Servant because she gave me the gift of the first gaze. There is no thought of refusing such a gift, even if I do not understand the nature of it. I left everything and everyone I loved to be here with her, and to teach her. What I am to teach her, I know not. I may never know. She certainly doesn't know, or at least she has not told me. I will never see my mother again because Nuala blessed me with her gaze. Some days, it is hardly a blessing.

'Where you and I differ is that you understand the *why* of what you do. I do not. I know that several of the Walking- and Wrist-Servants see my job as easier than their own. If they only knew the mental energy it takes to keep up with her roiling brain, they would not wish for a day in my shoes.'

She is quiet. Have I said too much? I instantly regret my candour this early in our friendship.

'Teacher-Servant, thank you for explaining it to me in those terms. I was naive to think that being inside Nuala's head would be reward enough. But to work without purpose. That I find difficult to understand.'

'You yourself told her the story of the destruction of the Great City by a former Puppet Queen who felt her purpose had been served. I suspect these tales are merely used to frighten or delight children at bedtime, but they are enough to keep us serving, although we know not why. I have attempted to find meaning in the Service itself, rather than trying to discover the reason for it. I suspect there are those Servants of lesser imagination who do not question the work, but who simply carry it out. I further suspect it is they who resent me, and the relative lack of physical labour my position requires. But what of you?'

'You know that my mother is elderly, and that I came from the City Across the Waters to be with her and care for her. While I'm glad I'm here to help her, I miss my life there. I was a teacher in that city. How strange. You a teacher here, and me now a sewing girl.' She gives a little laugh.

'Perhaps you may one day be a teacher here as well. There are many children in this city, and we always have a shortage.'

'That is a fine thought, Teacher-Servant. And some day I may look into it. While my mother is alive, though, I like the mindless nature of the work I do. This way, I can be completely available to her. And perhaps occasionally win a game against her! She is a formidable player the rare times we follow the rules.'

'I envy you your ability to see your mother each week. I wish...Well, as I often tell Nuala, wishing for something does not make it happen. Shall we have more ale?'

She winks at me over her mug, and my insides spill.

'I could become very pleasantly drunk with you this after-noon, Teacher-Servant.'

Each time we visit, the young woman passes me a cup of hot tea as I sit on Nuala's shoulder, and she and the older woman engage me in light chat. The young woman sits in her chair on her balcony and we pass the time in pleasant conversation as Nuala looks into the room she loves.

'Teacher-Servant, I know there are other young Giants like Nuala in the City of Servants. Are there many?'

I sip this special blend of tea I am growing to love in the place I feel most at home. The young woman's mother whispers stories to her, and shows her the book of which she has become so fond.

'Yes,' I tell the young woman. 'In the City of Servants, there are many giants—young and old—fashioned of wood and metal, but no one can identify which will display a woodlight. Most will remain inanimate, and those are the giants we practice upon when we are training for the Service. I am fortunate in that this one awoke at my touch and my voice.'

'What an honour it must be for you, Teacher-Servant! I can tell you that many of my friends think you the luckiest man alive. I do remember our conversation, but to be permitted to ride with her, help her learn, to know what she thinks and feels. All of this is unknown to us, and we must trust you to tell us these things and how she...'

'Teacher-Servant! Tell her how I love her and how much I desire to be small enough to sit in her small home and tell her...'

'Nuala! Just because the young woman cannot hear you, it does not mean that you may thrust your thoughts upon me while I am having a discussion with her. You must learn to be polite. Have I not asked this of you repeatedly?'

My sharp tone brings the young woman to her feet. 'I have an idea,' she says. 'Teacher-Servant, may I please spell a word for Nuala upon the game board?'

'Of course. That is a marvellous idea, and very kind of you.' My nod tells her she has not overstepped, but that caution is in order.

She places her teacup and saucer on the balcony table and enters the flat. She brings out the word game and the velvet bag, pours the tiles with the letters upon them out onto the word board. P and K tick to the floor and she retrieves them. She moves her fingers through the tiles, turning them up to reveal the ones she needs. As she finds them, she lays them out on the board.

'What does it say, Teacher-Servant? What *word* does she spell?' The wood of Nuala's earlobe heats my thigh in a frantic burst of desire.

'Patience, my beloved.' Though the young woman cannot hear them, I am embarrassed by Nuala's childlike outbursts, and feel myself turning red.

'Do you see, Nuala? The kind young woman is showing you a word. Shall we sound it out together? Beloved, it says, GIANT.'

'Giant. That is what *I* am!'

'Teacher-Servant, may I touch Nuala's hand?'

Though I would like to refuse her, there is no way to do it. She is cunning in asking to touch Nuala in her presence— Nuala would never let me forget if I did not permit this. I call out, 'Right-arm Wrist-Servants. Please raise Nuala's right hand to the window.' Gently, gently, they do so, and Nuala's hand hovers above the balcony, the long fingers far enough away not to damage the glass doors. The young woman touches the back of Nuala's great, immobile hand, the fingers forever unable to grasp those of the young woman who strokes the wood at Nuala's knuckles.

'Be careful you do not get a splinter. Her Wrist-Servants sanded her this morning,' I say, 'but she sometimes has rough spots.'

My friend looks at me. 'I'm not worried. I've had splinters before.'

She touches Nuala's hand as I reach into Nuala's mind. All has gone quiet. I am alarmed for a moment as I can hear nothing, sense nothing. The young woman caresses Nuala's hand, touching each of her unmoving fingers with her own small and supple ones. Then, after a slight pause, Nuala's thoughts to me are a torrent of questions about hands and tea. About why—if she is in command—she may not drink tea if she desires it. This flurry is followed by thoughts of the young woman's touch. How soft and loving the hands of the young woman are! How it would be if the young woman were to close her eyes for her and tell her a story. How I looked across a table at the young woman in a room Nuala does not recognize.

'And the word, Teacher-Servant! The word. She spelled GIANT for me. She knows that I am a Giant. Now I know the word *Giant*. Perhaps I shall soon know all the words!'

I do my best to ride out the waves of Nuala's thoughts as they crash around inside my head. The realization that Nuala kept from me her knowledge of my meeting with our young woman.

I collect myself. 'You have been most kind today in showing my Nuala a word on your game board. I am in your debt.'

'Teacher-Servant, you are not. It gives me great pleasure to see you and Nuala so frequently. Please come again next week.'

I laugh. 'I'm not sure I could prevent it!'

Astride Nuala's shoulder, I filter out her most passionate thoughts. I take hold of the braid I wove for her so that I may close my eyes without being thrown from her body at a sudden turn of her torso. The young woman's touch. So gentle and loving. The warmth of the tiny human hand wasted on the wood of the unmoving fingers of my charge, her inability to appreciate the meaning of fingers caressing her.

'I burn to be free of the Engine behind me, Teacher-Servant. I know it is there, but I cannot see it. I know that I cannot move without it. You have told me so. It does not feel anything for me, though it helps me wake and walk. I know it helps me to bend down so that I can see inside the room of the woman I love. I want to walk on my own, but I am not permitted! Why?'

'Nuala, I have told you time and time again that the Engine and your Servants are what enable you to move.'

We are on one of our daylong walks around the city. The walks about which the Servants have begun to question me: 'Why do we do this every day? What is the point?' they want to know, and their questions are not unreasonable. I tell them that unless and until Nuala chooses to reveal the answers to me, I have none to give. All I know is that this walking—this same route—is what she desires.

I feel their lack of confidence in me, in my answers. Of what use is my job if all I do is listen to Nuala's thoughts without sharing them with anyone? Truly, most of her thoughts are not worth sharing, and I have tried to articulate this to my colleagues, to no avail. They think I'm dissembling, and that I am hiding key information from them for reasons of my own.

But what point would there be in telling them she wants to drink tea and visit trees, and that her thoughts are no more profound or interesting than that? Wouldn't they think that just *anyone* could do my job? Perhaps they would be right.

Nuala bursts into my thoughts. 'Teacher-Servant, I have heard the Engine's great metal grindings, and I have smelled the fuel that makes it churn and push me forward. Why am I commanded to love a noisy Engine that I cannot see? Do I not rule here? I would like it very much if you would tell the Engine at once to let me go, and let me be small so that I can lie on the floor of the room of my beloved young woman. She will bring me the word game and she will spell NUALA. That word—my name—will be for me.'

'You must watch your haughty tone, young lady.'

She instantly quiets her mind.

'Beloved, you know what you ask is not possible. You are the size you are, and no amount of wishing will make you small. You know this. You are a Giant, and you have woken into a world that is too small for you.'

'I only want her to take me in her arms,' she says. 'Her arms are smaller than mine, and she cannot embrace me as another Giant could. A Giant friend. My young woman would do the best she could with her tiny, city-person arms. I could pretend that her tiny arms are Giant arms, and that her small arms of flesh and blood could go all around the oak of me. Her arms would make me able to drink tea. Her hands would tamper with the nails at my mouth, so that I might speak to her. My arms would turn her into metal and wood.'

'Little one, it is fine to have thoughts like these, but it is important that you learn the difference between what you would like, and what must be. Sometimes they are not the same.'

I cannot hear her.

'Little one, you are permitted a visit to your trees tomorrow, should you wish it. Before you answer me, know that you must make a choice. We can either visit the young woman and the word game, or we can visit the trees. We cannot do both in one day.'

After her thoughts eddy and twist, which I imagine would cause her pain if she could feel it, she says, 'My trees.'

So she has chosen. And so it shall be.

In my dream I see myself, my head tilted back to receive this warmth, this hot shower. I am naked, and I am made of wood and metal. There are cables before my eyes, and a long serpentine arm is lodged in my lower back, its fingers around my spine. After I am cleansed, Nuala floats up to my lips and dries them with a thick white towel. She is made of flesh, her blood sings in her, and she dries me, her hand in my hair. She gives me a gentle kiss, but I cannot return it. Strings and pulleys, wires and rope hem me in. We walk through our city, my Nuala and I. I cannot move on my own, and my arms and legs are lifted and lowered by tiny people far below. On my shoulder sits a small girl of flesh and blood. She whispers the secrets and stories of my city to me.

Amost profound silence. She is closed to me, but for a despair that threatens to tear my heart from my body. Today, I let her stand with her tree until the sun had nearly set, and the Servants had grown restless. Her hair in the breeze, rippling against the needles and cones of the trees surrounding her, loving her. Her eyes closed, her cheek against the trunk she embraced.

I do not know what they said to one another. If Nuala could weep, I believe she would have.

Sap clings to her cheek where she laid it against the tree she loves best. The tree that gave of itself to her. I have given her nothing. I do my best to wipe her face clean with the corner of my handkerchief, but my own hands become sticky. The front of her dress is a mess of viscous amber and needles. My hair catches in a drop of sap at her earlobe, and I must pull it free.

I awaken in the dead middle of the night, overcome by love and tears. Nuala is dreaming. She walks through the city without the Engine, her back straight and tall. She has no Servants and is free to move about as she wishes. No cables cage her vision, and I am nowhere to be seen.

The freedom she is granted! I rise from my bed, shivering at the intensity of her desire. She sees herself as small as the human woman in the game-and-tea room, and she climbs a ladder to the young woman's home. The woman waits for her on the other side of the door. She is no longer flesh and blood, but is made of oak and rivets.

Our young woman takes my Nuala into her arms, and Nuala is small enough to fit there. She wraps her whole self around Nuala, wood against wood, Nuala's knotted face nestled into the metal of the young woman's throat. Is there no end? When will she awaken? My head roars with it.

Now she is Giant again, and she and the young woman— made Giant as well—stride hand-in-hand to the edge of the Great City. They look out over the waters. They wait at the edge of the green forest Nuala knows lies beyond the cemetery.

I wrap my robe around me against the early autumn chill and set the kettle to boil. It is pointless attempting a return to my own slumber as long as this night-passion seizes my Puppet Queen. As long as every grain in the slats that make up her chest pulse with desire for the word-loving young woman and the Land of Giants. Oh, why did I tell her of that place?

She looks out across the green expanse to find the Giants coming to claim her, to welcome her to the Land of Giants.

They can hear one another and speak with mouths that are not nailed shut. Nuala's joy bursts through the branches inside her, their leaves sparking to green and vivid life. The trees are alive, their arms thrown open to her. She holds her own arms wide and the Giants and the trees crowd around her, touch her hair, help her loosen her closed jaw.

Finally, the dream is over, but it has awakened Nuala. It is not yet dawn, but I must go to her. I am doubled over at her groaning hopelessness to find that she is unable to move, was merely dreaming. I set out, in a paroxysm of resentment and stumbling, clutching my side where her emptiness at the lost Giant arms seems most acute.

She calls me. 'Where are you?'

'I'm coming, my love. Be brave, little one.' I reach her side, climb her cheek, and open one great eye, so that she may see me. I sit cross-legged on her cheek and lean against her nose.

'Oh, Teacher-Servant. I know I was dreaming, but if only my dream was not a dream. If only it were real. I must tell you...'

'You needn't, beloved. For remember, your thoughts are my thoughts: your dreams mine.'

'But I was free, Teacher-Servant. Free and in the arms of Giants. The ones you have told me of! They must be real! How else could I dream of them?'

'Little one,' I tell her, running my hands down her nose from bridge to tip, the gesture warm, repetitive, and soothing. 'You must remember that not all that we dream is true or real. Why, just last night, I dreamt—as I often do—that I was made of wood and metal! Isn't that silly?'

My tone and fingertips calm her thoughts, her wild dream-desires, and her left eye twitches. I close the lid and resume my gentle stroking of the bridge of her nose, clearing my own mind as I soothe her back to sleep, to dream—I hope—of nothing for a few more hours.

Just to be alone. Just for an hour, to be inside my own thoughts without Nuala's crowding me as the Giants crowded her in her dream.

I shall lose my mind.

We Servants take a few moments to rest outside the alehouse. The proprietor brings us tankards, frothy and chilled. We recline, hot and fatigued, against Nuala's ankle.

'The monotony!' says a Right Wrist-Servant, clinking his glass against mine.

'Shh! She can hear our every word.'

'Teacher-Servant,' he says, 'unless you have taught her the word *monotony*, how would she know it? Perhaps she thinks it is a love word. Don't think we haven't noticed you tell us nothing of what she thinks.'

'I can promise you her thoughts would not interest you.'

'Perhaps we might like to find that out for ourselves. You are *her* teacher, not ours. I hope you haven't overestimated the importance of your position, Teacher-Servant. You are not the same man I knew in the City of Servants.' He rises to finish the beer with his fellow Wrist-Servants.

The

lift and fall of her feet on pavement and stone. The sounds her knees make as the winds whistle through them. Hem of her red dress swishing around her thighs, and Servants, always Servants, raising, lowering, grunting, jumping. Keeping her walking.

'Teacher-Servant, it pleases me to see my Servants working so hard for me. Is the gift of my gaze truly the only gift they require in return for their service to me?'

From where I ride, I see the joy on the newest Walking-Servant's face, in stark contrast to the dissatisfaction and fatigue on the face of the next one in line to lift the great leg. There are those who thought the Service would bring never-ending joy and fulfillment. Others, like the Kitchen-Servants, know that sometimes the tedium is nearly too much to bear.

'My Nuala, you have seen the Servants eating lunch and drinking tea, have you not? Each of your Servants is housed, fed, and clothed well, and we all receive a small amount of goods with which to barter for personal things we might desire. These provisions are writ down in our lore, and we follow them still.'

'What do you most desire, Teacher-Servant?'

My wishes are never uppermost in her thoughts, and I stammer. 'Books, my love. All I want are books. You have seen some of your Servants reading books when they are not attending to their duties in your Service. The books they read are filled with words, and each book tells a story. Some are stories of far-off lands, and some are the stories of their own lives: of the city people and of your Servants. I have everything else I need. Books and the gift of your gaze—are all I could ever desire.'

'I would like to find a book to give you,' Nuala says. 'I do not think it should be like the book the old woman shows to me. The one with only pictures. I think that you would like a book with many words. Perhaps one day when I can spell words, I will know the right book for you.'

'That would be perfect, my child, but you needn't give me anything beyond your love and your thoughts.'

The Servants have slowed outside the tavern. Here is where they take a break from the strenuous work of lifting and lowering great wooden legs, the back-and-forth swing of Giant forearms. They prepare to lift her into her afternoon sleeping chair, which stands down the street from the Servants' tavern. Her feet still, her hands lowered to her sides, she yearns to move again, but knows it is time for her nap.

The Engine pulls its thrusting snake from Nuala's spine and her mind relaxes for a moment. From above, the great arc of the Engine's long arm lifts her from the ground, me still on her shoulder. The Engine's act of lifting her frightens her nearly beyond thought. It is at this moment that she feels most conflicted and agitated, dangling by her head—helpless.

'What if it drops me, Teacher-Servant?'

I assure her that it will not. That she is firmly attached, safe. The Engine lowers her into the sleeping chair in which she will spend the next few hours. Head-Servant crawls atop her skull to undo the clasps that hold her in its grasp.

'Teacher-Servant, tell me again about the Land of Giants. Is it like the land I saw in my dream?'

'You would be lonely and afraid in the Land of Giants, little one. For Giants are like the people of the city. Some are kind and some are not, and you would need a protector to help you tell the difference.'

My Nuala is on the edge of sleep, but her thought-questions will not stop. 'But if we were together, Teacher-Servant?'

'That is impossible, beloved. You remember that I am not permitted to leave the Great City. It is a condition of my service.'

'But is not your service to me, wherever I am?'

I am chilled by the questions she asks, the conclusions she has recently begun to draw. I ruffle the edges of the book in my tunic pocket. How I yearn to read, but she will not give me even a few moments' peace.

I climb down the rope ladder to her lap, and step up the wooden one to her chin, my feet resting on the topmost wide step. I lean my hair against her lips. 'You must understand, my Nuala. In the Land of Giants, there are those who would wish you harm because of your beauty and your kind thoughts and your wise mind. This last most of all. I have seen the Land of Giants, and while it is more beautiful than you can imagine, it is terrible as well.'

'But do you not think, Teacher-Servant, that it is best I learn the ways of Giants from those of my own kind? After all, you are a wise teacher, but you are not a Giant. My word-giving young woman is all I think of, but she is not a Giant.'

I stroke her cool cheek, run my thumb over her lower lip, and I am overcome by the desire to shout at her, scold her, cause her pain by pulling the hair I unfailingly treat with delicacy and care.

How I yearn for one sentence, one thought from Nuala that does not conjure images of the young woman. A moment of freedom in which I could think of anything, anything except Nuala and her great obsession for the young woman.

'Let me tell you a story, Nuala. In the Land of Giants, you would know love as you never have here. Not even my devotion to you—greater than the devotion of all your Servants and the city people combined—could compare to the fervent passion a Giant feels for one of her own kind. You cannot love me or our long and lean young woman as you would love a Giant, for we are not Giants, as you have correctly noted, and cannot embrace you in the way of a Giant. We cannot kiss you with Giant, wooden lips, for our lips are soft and are made of flesh.

'Listen now. I have seen Giants in that Land, their huge, wooden arms around one another in embraces they are free to give and receive. They are free to roam and love howsoever they choose. Everything is Giant-sized for them. All the homes of the Giants are large enough so that no Giant ever has to bend to enter the dwelling of another. Even the teacups are the correct size for their Giant hands.'

The stirrings in her heart rumble through her chest and rattle me to my core: to the pinch in my own heart at my deception.

'Even the teacups! Are the Giants in the Land of Giants permitted to drink *hot tea*? To know how it tastes?'

'I am merely teasing you for being fixed on the idea of tea,' I tell her. 'Sometimes I do not want to know what goes on in that head of yours.'

When I kiss her, I can feel her burn with the heat of my story, the heat of the promises I cannot keep, words I work to make sure she believes, even though I know they are empty. Her lips are hot against mine. The metal of her throat is warm and pulsing as though tea had passed through its pulleys and gears. I climb down and sit in her lap, my back against her belly.

'There is no need to seek permission in the Land of Giants, Nuala. There, a Giant may eat and drink as she chooses. She may laugh and cry and speak and love as she wishes.' Her innards thrum against me, her mind full of waterfalls of tea.

'Sleep now, my Nuala,' I say. 'We shall resume our adventures when you awaken, but you are weary. I can hear it in your thoughts.'

'When may we go to the Land of Giants, Teacher-Servant?'

I wait until her breathing deepens and she is on the edge of dreaming.

'Never, my beloved.' As I step over Nuala's right hand, the wrist shifts beneath my feet. I catch myself before I fall, and climb to the ground, shaking.

While

she naps, I return to her bedroom and try to steady myself. The walls covered with things I had hoped she would come to love. Pictures of trees I have drawn for her these past few weeks. Pictures of other Giants I have never seen, but have imagined. The false giants I have tried to imbue—in my drawings—with a kind of life. Pictures I have drawn of her while she sleeps. I have taken my pencils in hand to draw her hair, her lips. I haven't the skill to capture the heaving worlds in her eyes.

The lies I have told her. I know nothing of the Land of Giants. I lie in her bed and touch this lock of my own hair. When we first arrived, I cut my long, curling hair, and placed it in a bowl my mother threw for me, both of us younger then. The uneven bowl is on the table next to Nuala's bed, so that she may smell me when night falls, and I have gone to my quarters to sleep. The timbre of my voice, the weight and warmth of my thighs as I sit on her shoulder, the fragrance of my hair: all these quiet her.

I am anything but quiet.

Nuala

says the more she sees the young woman, the more she senses that what is inside her—what she is made of—is twisted upon itself and burning. She awakens now from dreams of burning. Her knees and wrists on fire and unquenchable, her heart dripping molten steel onto the worn carpet of the young woman's small room, the seared joints of her great arms, black smoke curling above our burning bodies and billowing into the choking air. I stand at the window, reach to her through the flames. In her dreams, I burn as strongly as she. My lips on fire, my clothing turned to ash, melted to my roaring torso.

My rhythms and the depth of my sleep are poisoned by the flames of Nuala's dreaming. How to combat this. How to turn her mind. How not to succumb to the destruction of my own.

I am alone in the alehouse today. Senior Iron-Servant is repairing a tear in Nuala's dress and cannot join me. The rend is my fault. When I asked the Wrist-Servants to lower Nuala's arm from the young woman's flat, the fabric on her sleeve caught on the tip of an iron balcony-railing.

And when I climbed down from her wrist at yesterday's napping time, I knew that her wrist was secure. Yet I was not. I am sure-footed; my grey slippers know every rivet, every bolt of that wrist. But somehow I missed my step and nearly tumbled. No cable was chained to it, no joint turned by any Servant. I take a long drink of my ale and blame my clumsiness. After all, is not Senior Iron-Servant always telling me I was prone to tripping and falling when I was a boy? I could not be trusted to bring the Iron-Servants a tray of water and biscuits for fear I would spill it! Has this lack of balance followed me into my middle years? It must be so.

I practice shielding my thoughts from Nuala. The tavern noise seeps into my head, and the din of talking and laughter blocks her most effectively. Added to this are the pleasantly deadening effects of the ale. I am as close to peace as I've been in some time.

Two young Walking-Servants enter the tavern and move toward me. 'Teacher-Servant!' one calls. 'May your joy be trebled in the Service. Do you mind if we sit down?'

'And yours as well! Please, I should be most grateful for your company,' I reply, and stand to turn out two chairs for the young women. They cannot have forty years combined. I am an old man alongside them, and I tug my long hair forward where it shows at its most youthful and flattering.

'I have noticed your hard work on the ground, lifting and lowering Nuala's legs,' I tell them, and turn to signal the server for another pitcher of ale and two more mugs. 'You do drink ale, do you not?'

'Oh heavens, yes,' sighs the one with blonde locks as long and curly as my own, her limbs relaxing in anticipation of the cool tonic. 'I think you know how hard it is lifting those legs all day. This is what we signed up for, but where else can we whine about it except in the tavern?' We laugh, pour, and touch our tankards together. 'To exercise!'

'You work hard on the ground, and do not think I am not grateful to you,' I say. 'It is difficult for me to express my thanks while we are walking, and truthfully, I often think some of the Servants do not feel I work as hard as they do. But keeping up with Nuala's thoughts and desires is more than a full-time job.'

Careful, Teacher-Servant, I tell myself. You do not know these young women well. 'But that is not a subject for a most pleasant sharing of afternoon ale!'

'We find your work fascinating, Teacher-Servant,' the quieter of the two says. 'How did you know that you were chosen? What did it feel like?' The girls—for I can only call them that in relation to myself—lean in, elbows on the sticky table.

'How to describe the gift of the first gaze. You have felt it in the mornings, yes?'

'I've never experienced anything like it,' the young, curly-haired one says. 'I felt like my insides had been...but how was it for you?'

I collect my words before they tumble out of me to these two girls full of questions. 'Do you remember being in the City of Servants and walking among the great rows of unawake giants? Can you call to mind the feeling of wanting one to wake as you climbed its ladder, to be given the gift of its first gaze?'

'Of course we can,' says the quieter one, with dark hair on her head and on the strong muscles of her forearms. 'However, no one was blessed but you.'

'You remember the ladders we climbed each morning, the rows upon rows of sleeping giants we tried to wake by lifting the left eyelid. The crush of sadness when the eye returned only an emptiness, void of life or recognition. How the Master-Servants made sure we started on a new row each morning, so as to avoid an unnatural bond between one of us and a sleeping giant.'

'Yes,' says the dark-haired one. 'I do recall one hopeful Servant talking to a false giant morning after morning, which she knew we were not allowed to do. She knew that speaking to a sleeping giant could cause it to awaken under false pretences, especially if the Servant was speaking of a love she could not yet truly feel.'

'That's right. When I first climbed to Nuala's face, I did not know her name, and by then I was resigned to my belief that none of the giants would awaken in my lifetime. Why should they? No one could remember a time in which a living Giant was awake. Or worse: I feared a sleeping giant would awaken to someone else, thus ensuring the rest of us a life of Service to the new Giant, but not a life of love.

'When I opened Nuala's eye and she gave me the gift of her first gaze, I could not breathe. But it was imperative that I hold eye contact with her. Otherwise, she might have made her eye opaque and empty again, and waited for someone more deserving. In that moment, I felt a pull from her body to mine. As though a Giant hand had reached into my chest and quickened my heartbeat. My tears spilled and landed on her face, but I was too timid to wipe them off, and they rolled from her eyes into her hair as though they were her own.

'I cannot explain why she chose me, but perhaps she knew my mind was malleable enough to accept her thoughts. They began penetrating me the moment she became aware, starting with her telling me her name. When she did, the Two Great Secrets were given to me alone. Nuala knows nothing of them. Wait, I've said too much. I'm boring you!'

'No!' says the curly-haired one. 'That feeling! That's exactly why we joined the Service. I want to feel that. I can't tell you...'

The quiet one says nothing, and looks at me with what seems like wariness. I do not blame her. My story is fantastic, and those who have not received the gift of the first gaze—and I am the only one in living memory—must be sceptical.

'If I understand the lore correctly,' I tell them, 'I am one in a long line of Teacher-Servants to a long line of Giants stretching past into time no one can bring to mind, and of which our records are mythical at best. No one is old enough to remember another living Giant before Nuala—except those who are now too old to have a clear recollection of anything. And yet the stories passed down tell us there must have been others.'

'Of course we know these stories,' says the outspoken one. 'We can't join the Service until we do, as you know, but we know nothing of the Two Great Secrets. We know it is not our right to ask you about them, so we won't embarrass you by enquiring. And it all makes sense to us. What are the chances of none of the unawake giants ever waking before Nuala?'

'It's a frightening thought,' says the other. 'What would that first Giant have done to make us have to obey *this* Giant's thoughts and wishes?'

'That is a fair question, and again, the answers lie in lore. They say there was a benevolence in that giant. A peacefulness in her rule that perhaps we are to nurture in Nuala. Honestly, I do not know,' I say, and signal for more ale.

'Oh, no thank you, Teacher-Servant. We want to return to our quarters and change into clean uniforms before the waking time this afternoon. Just look at the patches of sweat on these ones! They need laundering.'

'Very well. I thank you for your company. You may find me at this table most afternoons, with ale before me, for truly it is the only way...' I look into my mug. 'It is the only way to prepare myself for Nuala's endless questions when she awakens.'

'We bid you good day, Teacher-Servant, and may your joy be trebled in the Service.'

'And yours as well.' And they are gone. Oh, for friendly company like this on all my lonely afternoons! Despite their absence, I order another pitcher of ale, and two fresh mugs. Perhaps I will have more company today.

I know I will not.

'But when shall I drink hot tea from a Giant-sized teacup, Teacher-Servant?' Nuala asks as we walk through the city on our accustomed route to the home of the young woman.

'Never, if you don't stop asking.'

She is quiet. I cannot read her. My heart drops into my pelvis. How dare I?

'I am sorry, my dearest Nuala. I was cross with you for simply being yourself. For being curious. Can you forgive my outburst?'

'I do not understand what it is to *forgive*, Teacher-Servant, but you seem sad for speaking sharply toward me. I shall try not to pester you with so many questions.'

'No, my love.' I entangle myself in her hair. 'Do not hide your thoughts from me. For this is why I exist. To hear your thoughts, to understand how you grow and learn, to find out why you are awake to us, and to grant that which you desire.'

While her head is turned from me, she says, 'If your existence were based on granting me my desires, then you should not exist. For I have not had hot tea. And I doubt I ever shall.'

I will not quarrel with her. Astride her great shoulder is where we are most compatible, where we do not fight, where she has the fewest questions and comes near to contentment.

'I would be grateful if you could forget how my tone stung you, Nuala.'

'Yes, Teacher-Servant, I can forget.'

From this height, I see my city anew every day. I have my handle, but if I need support, I prefer to hold the collar of her red dress or the braid I have woven in her hair.

'Your eyes, my lovely, are the eyes of night and the eyes of the day. The eyes of city streets and the small people who walk them. You have seen them from high, high above, and I see them from atop your shoulder.'

'How do I see, Teacher-Servant?'

'When you awoke, it was most important to find out whether you could see. We learned that you could because you gave me the gift of your first gaze, a gift for which I shall always be grateful. You are a complex creature, my Nuala. It needn't be important to you how you see, only *that* you see.

'The tiny people look terribly small down there, don't they, Nuala? Almost like insects, running about, laughing in groups, swaying against one another with drink and song and talk and seeing what little there is to see from so low down.'

'They seem rather happy doing the things city people do,' she says. 'When they turn their faces to look up at me, I see what I think must be happiness there.'

'I was once one of the small people, Nuala. Before I became your Teacher-Servant.' I tell her that I have lived that life, the company of only the thoughts within one's head, the life of cold drinks and conversations and desire and cruelty passing for love. The comfort of bodies my own size.

She says, 'I see some waving at you from their places far, far below. Do you miss being one of the people of the ground, Teacher-Servant?'

'No, my Nuala. For you conferred upon me the title of Teacher-Servant. This is the highest honour a Servant may receive. For only I may speak with you, only I may hear your thoughts, answer your questions, kiss your cheeks, and tell you stories. I am blessed indeed.'

After

we have visited the young woman and her mother, I instruct the Servants to allow Nuala to remain standing for a time down the street from the tavern, and to leave the two of us to our conversation. A Walking-Servant climbs over the arms of the Engine and passes me three bottles of ale.

'What is she thinking about this evening, Teacher-Servant?'

'You know I needn't tell you.'

'Fine. But it's been a long time since you've joined us, and we miss your company. We're going to the alehouse. Come fetch us when it's time to put her to bed. Better yet, stay and have a glass of ale *before* it's time.'

I settle into Nuala's hair. She does not mind standing still for a while and does not feel the air's crisp bite as sharply as I do. She is more amenable to standing if I am seated upon her, and will tell her story after story.

'Your friends miss you, Teacher-Servant,' Nuala says. 'As I think my mother must miss me, although I do not remember her. I think that I have seen mothers with young ones at their sides. One seems to be the mother, as the older lady in the little blue room seems to be the mother of our young woman. Who was my mother, Teacher-Servant?'

'You may have had a mother once, Nuala. Of this I cannot be sure. I had one once. I have not seen her since I moved here to the Great City to love and serve you.'

'Tell me of the Mother-Giant, Teacher-Servant.'

'Perhaps she kissed you once, and you no longer remember. Perhaps she swore to you that she would never leave you, and then she did. Perhaps you remember someone smoothing the longing from your brow, the brush of wooden lips on the cool of your child-cheek, the smell of oil and laundry, of sap and pine on your Mother's breath. Perhaps this happened, but you do not remember the when of it.'

'Teacher-Servant, you torture me so. I long to hear stories of the Mother, although I cannot fully understand. The pictures you draw in my mind with your words make me wish and wish for such a Giant.'

'A false mother-giant lies in the City of Servants, little one. I may not take you there, so please do not think of asking. You must trust me when I say that she is not alive and cannot love you.'

'What is the City of Servants, Teacher-Servant?'

'Would you like me to tell you?' Her earlobe warms, and she thinks me a yes. She is growing weary and will soon want to be released for the night, but my second ale is making its cold, slow way down my gullet. It tastes bitter tonight, and brings me no pleasure.

I'll give her the painful stories if that's what she wants.

'In the City of Servants are many false giants. Some are in the form of girls such as you, and some are in the shape of mothers and aunts. No one knows who made them, or why they lie there. They've always been there. They lie in great rows inside long, low buildings, one next to another, eyes and minds closed. They are dressed, and their hair is brushed and plaited. They sleep under great blankets awaiting the awakening touch, and the people of the City of Servants walk among them each morning in the hopes that one will awaken.

'We never knew when one of the false giants might arise. No one had seen it happen until I opened your left eye and you chose me as your Teacher-Servant. They say that some of the false giants have slept there for centuries: longer than anyone could imagine. We kept them clean and oiled and free from dust and the moths that would chew their dresses to tatters if we permitted them to.

'In the City of Servants, where I was born, we were taught from a very young age how to serve the Giant we might perhaps one day meet. All our lives, we were schooled on wood and metal. We learned the exacting movements of wrists and throats and eyes. The giant upon which we trained was a false one: a tall and lifeless structure, which did not love or yearn or want to play word games. Inside the false giant, wires moved and pulleys pulled ropes, but there was nothing like wonder, and no signs of a mighty oak. The Engine kept the false giant straight and tall for our lessons. When the false giant moved, it was not with curiosity such as yours. It was simply the mechanics of the Engine and the future Servants manipulating the wooden arms and face of the false giant who saw nothing.'

'Could the false giant not lie down and dream?'

'There was no need to do so, little one, for the false giant felt nothing. No love, no fatigue, no curiosity or fear. No sleep, no seeing, and no dreaming.

'As we grew into men and women, we each found out how we best served the false giant. Some of the future Servants were skilled at helping the false giant move its arms. If they were fortunate and worked hard, they would become Wrist-Servants if one of the false giants awoke.' I have finished my third beer and I crave another, but there is no one to bring me one.

'Some found they liked to help the false giant lift its legs, and they learned how to create the motion you see the Walking-Servants use when we walk through the city.'

'Why did you desire to become Teacher-Servant of the long, long hair?'

'My mother was proud of my long, curling hair. There was no hair like it in all the city, she used to say. She took special care to keep it clean and to tie it with a ribbon. As I grew up, the Master-Servants noticed that I kept my hair well, and that I liked to plait the lifeless hair of the false giant. I would speak to it and tell it stories as I worked with its hair and face, making up tales I thought might amuse it, were it alive.

'Because of my imagination and knowledge, when my training was complete, the Master-Servants gave me the honour of being your Teacher-Servant when I met you. But only if—when you awakened for the first time and cast your eyes upon me—you gave me the gift of your first gaze. If you had met my eyes with indifference, or had not awoken at all, a Servant more clearly in your favour would have replaced me.'

The ale has loosened my tongue. 'The depth of my gratitude paralyzes me, Nuala. Though you could not have known you were giving me the greatest gift by casting your new eyes upon my humble face, I thank you regardless. For the chance to love you and serve you.'

'But do they still train Servants in the City of Servants?' she asks, her weariness a palpable weight. I must let my beloved sleep.

'Yes, Nuala. The false giant stands there still, I am told, though I've not returned since you awoke.'

'But I have all the Servants I require, do I not?' If Nuala could yawn, she would, so overpowering is her weariness. 'They needn't keep training them, need they?'

Though she is standing, she is close enough to sleep that I feel no need to answer her, and I know she will not remember in the morning. I kiss her earlobe and whisper that I will fetch the Servants who put her to bed at night.

I climb down the ladders and make my way to the alehouse, where my colleagues said they would be. There is no one there and the doors are locked.

The hour is late, and I'm shivering. I do not realize how late it is until I find a slightly drunken Head-Servant leaning against Nuala's leg when I return to her.

'This is unacceptable, Teacher-Servant. We need sleep just as much as she does. I've told the others to join us here momentarily so we may put Her Majesty to bed, whether you will it or no.'

'I have my reasons for keeping her awake this late, Head-Servant. Reasons I needn't share with you. Your task is not to label my decisions *unacceptable*, but to follow my instructions.'

When the other Servants arrive, I receive the derisive, ale-soaked glances I deserve for allowing Nuala to stand well into the night, and for postponing the sleep of my fellow Servants. I take their censure with my head held high. I am Teacher-Servant, and I decide what she does and what time she goes to bed. For she is mine.

'Nuala

would very much like to hold one of your teacups,' I tell our young woman this morning. 'She is filled with the need to do so, both for herself and to witness the pleasure she imagines you will feel when you see her holding it. I am afraid she will never settle down until she is allowed to hold one. I understand the personal nature of one's possessions and I have explained to her that if you say no, she is not to argue or whimper. Is this not so, Nuala?'

Nuala's eyes are fixed on the tea things in the glass cupboard. But now she turns her eyes to the young woman and thought-whispers me, 'Yes, Teacher-Servant.'

'I would be delighted to allow Nuala to hold a teacup if this is what she wants.' She laughs. 'Who knows the workings of the girl's mind, Teacher-Servant? Imagine being so focused on such a small thing. Excuse me a moment.'

While the young woman chooses a cup, I have a Wrist-Servant turn Nuala's right hand so that her palm lies facing the sun. The Wrist-Servant secures the position of Nuala's hand and extends it toward the window so that the young woman will not place herself in danger by leaning too far to give Nuala the cup.

'You must be careful, Nuala. This does not belong to you. You are allowed to hold it only for a short time. Do you understand?'

I turn to the young woman. 'She is ready.'

The young woman has chosen a pretty cup, splashy with red roses. She places it in Nuala's outstretched palm. It sits in her hand as though it were made for that purpose. Nuala moves her eyes to it, taking in the beauty of the tiny thing she holds: its fragility and sheen.

'Teacher-Servant, it is so small. I almost cannot feel it in my hand. But I see it. It is the most beautiful thing I have ever seen. How grateful I am to the young woman.'

'You know what to do to show your thanks, Nuala.'

She gives the owner of the teacup the gift of her gaze, and the young woman answers the gift with a gaze of her own. Nuala returns her eyes to the treasure in her fingers. The Wrist-Servant has begun to tug. I call down. 'Hold steady, Wrist-Servant!' He struggles to keep Nuala's hand in place. She pulls it closer to her face, despite his best efforts.

A snap in the cable tethering Nuala's hand in Wrist-Servant's powerful grip. A cry from below as the slashing metal strikes his forearm. The teacup falls to the balcony and shatters as Nuala's arm crashes to her side, tangled in cables, dangling. My heart stops in my chest.

'Oh, Teacher-Servant!' Nuala's cry pierces my thought. 'She must not walk! Make her stop! I do not want her to cut her pretty feet on the broken pieces!'

'We are so sorry,' I tell my friend. 'Nuala, you understand that this cup cannot be repaired. You must say you are sorry that you broke this precious thing.'

She will not. She says nothing. I hear nothing.

'Nuala says she is so very sorry. I promise you that nothing like this will happen again. If you did not permit us to visit you again, I would understand.'

'Teacher-Servant, I have far too many teacups. I need three at most for your visits. I shall not miss this one. Nuala, do not worry.' She bends to pick up the largest shards. Her hand shakes as she collects the pieces. 'Will her hand be all right?'

My innards scream for Nuala to apologize. Vile thought-words skip from my mind to hers before I can harness them. My own thoughts run loose. Unmoored and shrieking.

'I have learned that my hands are too large to fit inside the blue room of the young woman,' Nuala says when I ask the lesson on our walk home.

'Your hands *are* too large, Nuala, but you must also understand that when we hurt someone, or break something that someone loves, we must show remorse, even if we did not intend to hurt the person or break her teacup.'

'I broke the teacup, Teacher-Servant, but I think I broke my beloved young woman as well. Never have I felt such a cracking inside of me. Will I topple, Teacher-Servant? Do I still have your love?'

'I've told you that nothing can topple you, Nuala. As for my love, doubt everything else in your city, in your world, and in your life. But do not doubt that. My love for you is in a place we call a *heart*. You do not have one, Nuala. Wood and metal beings do not have hearts.'

'My arms and legs are filled with broken wood, Teacher-Servant. You say I am made of a great tree, but now that I have broken the teacup, my strength-tree is splintered and burnt. The damaged and broken branches leave no room for what you call a *heart*.

'My hands will never be the right size, Teacher-Servant. Not for my young woman. I cannot make them small, nor can I make the young woman's hands Giant and wooden like my own. Your hands would fit inside the young woman's hands, as you are both small people.

'Your hands fit inside a warm room, and they can hold teacups without breaking them. You can stand inside a room and fit all of you inside it. I cannot do these things because I am a Giant, and Giants must not have teacups and word games.'

'Nuala, your hand moved against my wishes today. We must speak of this. You must remember that it is your Servants and the Engine who make you move. You must promise me that there will be no more acts of carelessness. You are not free to move on your own. What happened with your hand was an accident of your mechanics, and you must forever clear your mind of this desire. Such movement will never be yours to execute.'

'Am I to know nothing? Am I allowed to have nothing of my own, Teacher-Servant? Not even my own hands? I have my red dress and this pretty braid you fashioned for me, and I have my trees, but am I to have nothing else? Am I not to have anything that is large enough for my eyes and for my hands? May I not have a teacup of my own? How I long to hold something that is made for my hands.'

'Hush! Or you shall never have these things. I must also tell you that one of your Wrist-Servants was hurt because of your thoughtless movement.'

'What do I care for my Wrist-Servants?'

'Nuala, I am ashamed of you. Do you think of nothing but your own desire? You must learn to control yourself, or you shall never have the things you want.'

We walk home in silence, the only sound the running of cables through pulleys, the give of metal, the heaving of air in and out of the Servants' lungs, Nuala's right arm dangling at her side until she is safely asleep and the cables can be repaired. Huffs of steam from the Engine impaled in her back.

Senior

Wrist-Servant slams his ale tankard on the tavern tabletop, his left arm in a sling. 'I won't be able to work for a week! Were you sleeping up there, Teacher-Servant? You sit on high, whispering to Nuala, while the rest of us are down on the ground, broken cables whipping around our heads like snakes let loose. And for what? A teacup!'

'It is *you* who are to blame!' I stab the air in front of his face. 'Why did you not check the cables before we walked?'

'How dare you accuse me of negligence?' He tones down his bellowing, aware of eyes upon us. 'You know I check those cables morning and night. As I have done since you and I were young together in the City of Servants. And you rant at me now, when we both know...'

'Yes, yes. I apologize. It's all happened more quickly than we expected.' I finish my ale in one swallow. 'I will speak to Nuala, though to be frank with you, I am not sure what to say.'

'You'll find the words, Teacher-Servant.' His undeserved kindness sets me into a shiver. I reach across the table to clasp his good arm.

I pay for our ale with a book I know our server wants, and we take our leave of the proprietor. We walk the path to the scrap-yard, more slowly than we might ordinarily, as each step gives Wrist-Servant pain. He walks this path almost daily, digging for bits of iron, lengths of wood and scrap to repair the cracks and rends that Nuala presents him with. Today, though, the sling, a tired lag in his step.

In the scrapyard, Wrist-Servant finds the spiral coils he needs: thick, taut wires to repair the cables Nuala snapped when she moved—damn her—without my consent.

I barter some coffee for the rusted iron and bolts that Wrist-Servant requires.

Nuala

can think of nothing but shattering teacups and word games. Her child-mind—awake and asleep—surges with them. They splinter through my pores, porcelain smashes out of me, my eyes brittle red roses. I have no escape. She dreams the word GIANT in bursts of green-purple, the tiles fly above the game board, her arms detached from her body on the ground beside her. The teacups shatter, reassemble, shatter again. Shards litter the board and the word GIANT forms itself and the word rises eight, ten, eighty, a hundred tiles high. Teacups fall from the building the tiles have made. Bits of rose-stained cup land on the sleeves of Nuala's disembodied arms. Me frantic and pacing in my room for lack of sleep, the sound of Giant teacups breaking, deafening, my back rolled in shards, wooden tiles fall on me from great heights, bruising my shoulders. My hair sings with sharp and glistening slivers, fragments falling, dust to the floor of my wakeful room.

I sleep in fits and wake thinking of the pottery bowl I gave to Nuala. It sat so long on my own shelf, and now I miss it. I imagine removing it from her room, imagine that if she wondered for a day or two why the bowl had vanished, it might give me a moment's respite from her dreams of word games and the young woman of many letters. Yet I know her mind so well that should I take it back again, her dreams would be filled for days with images of thieves or Servants creeping into her room, removing things she knows are hers.

How quickly everything becomes hers! Me, the young woman, her Servants and their labours to make her move and see. How she claims all she sees! She would miss the bowl and ask me incessantly where it was until I broke. She would see the image of my mother who crafted it for me, who gave me her gift with a kiss. Nuala does not deserve to see my mind's picture of my mother.

How I long to see her. I know she is growing older as am I, but far away in the City of Servants, where each day she plaits a false giant's hair and keeps its clothes free of moths. Now that Nuala is awake, no other Giant will awaken until she is no longer Queen. Every future Servant knows this, but it is best not to think on it. Mother will remain at her post, lost to me, her life pointless until a new Giant awakens, and we doubt that will happen during our lifetime.

I cannot leave the Great City as long as I am Teacher-Servant, and she cannot come to me as long as Nuala is awake. I shall never see her again.

My books call to me in the few hours I am permitted to be alone, while Nuala sleeps in the afternoons, and when her dreams are calmer. I light a fire in the grate and scan the long, warped shelves, head tilted, look for my favourite volumes.

I pull *Tales of the Middle Worlds* from a low shelf, and my favourite poetic work: *Milks of Sea and Sand*. This purple velvet chair is the most comfortable memory of my life in the City of Servants.

The poetry is open on my lap, my tea steaming on the small table.

> *for when I see what lies beyond the boundary*
> *there will be no containment, my mind, my body, my wooden*
> > *thoughts*
> *a spill of longing from*

I drop the book to the floor. I cannot concentrate; her dreams are fists to my sternum in blasts of colour and noise. She dreams of her great feet, free of shoes, walking to the sea. She dreams of wading, and the waves created by her every step are large enough to drown five men my size.

Her mind shifts inside the dream, and now her trees are around her. She asks to see them daily. I can no longer deny her. The violence of her desire for them makes me tear my hair.

Then—of course—come the images of word games, embracing the young woman in wooden form. These so ubiquitous, so repetitious, I can almost block them. But my focus is lost. I must do something or go mad.

My heart clangs like the bells that wake my Nuala. I take the stairs up to the young woman's flat. I am losing my mind: that which makes me myself. If I am to ever have peace, this might be an answer.

She invites me to sit at her window and pours me a cup of tea. At my request, she reaches into the high cupboard above the teacups, her long muscles pushing the skin of her calves under the pink flowered dress as she rises to take down the game. She takes the purple velvet bag down and places it on the table, opening the board so its words face me.

My fingers hover. 'May I touch it?'

'Of course.' I open the bag and feel the cool wood. I pull out an A, two Ns, and a Q. She laughs. 'Not a very useful set of letters!'

I place the Q over a square that reads *Reveal Something*.

'You know that Nuala wishes nothing more than to play this word game. It is all she thinks of. And you, of course. I no longer have any thoughts of my own. Her dreams crowd mine. I am often able to filter her child-thoughts so that they do not overwhelm me, but I cannot do so with her thoughts of you. They are vivid and intimate.' I find my hand shaking, and put the cup and saucer on the table.

'Truly, my friend, I am exhausted and on the edge of despair. I fear Nuala's thoughts will be the only ones I shall have the rest of my days.'

The young woman turns to look out the open window, and a breeze from the street plays with her hair. She reaches into the bag. Draws out a W. Places it on a square that reads *Give of Yourself*.

'What can I do for you and Nuala, Teacher-Servant?' She sips her tea, her eyes on me.

I extract a G. I look around the board for an appropriate spot, and place the letter on a square reading *Risk It*. 'I ask if you would join Nuala's team of Servants. I would like you to supervise the building of a Giant word game for her. We have engineers and woodworkers to design and build the board. Your expertise in the painted tiles and the way in which the letters are used would be invaluable.

'Nuala desires little else, and as she points out to me, I have withheld so much from her. My hope is that with the word game at her hands, her thoughts will become focused, her mind less rattled as it grasps for the very thing she imagines she will never have.

'She dreams of being able to spell words, of learning to read. I realize you have employment in the sewing workshop and may not want to leave. You've made friends there, I know.'

She sets down an N. *Your Path is Clear*. 'I shall leave my work without thought,' she says. 'You know it gives me no pleasure. I'll simply tell my employer I've found more satisfying work.'

'But you know there is no purpose to this work. No real reason to do it. How will you find satisfaction in a job that does not allow you to know its purpose?'

'I'll be working with Nuala. And with you. That will be satisfaction enough.' She reaches across the table and puts her palm against mine. I hold the small warmth in my hands.

'Have you no wish to learn of your compensation?'

'None whatsoever,' she says, pulling her fingers from my grasp and standing to replace the letters and fold the board. 'I have my books and my word game. As long as I have lodgings and ample food and tea, there is nothing more for which

I cannot barter.' The matter is settled; the conversation is over. She takes the cup and saucer from me into her strong and steady hands. She kisses my lips, the teacup still warm between our bodies.

Over the next weeks, I breathe in the smell and sawdust of the oversized word game as it takes shape.

The Carpenter-Servants thrill to the change in their duties from repairing the chairs in the great dining hall, the small day-to-day details of fixing windowsills and sealing cracks in old salad bowls. To build something beautiful!

I am enchanted by the sounds of sandpaper and small handsaws, the crank of vice-grips holding jagged slabs of wood, each to be carved by hand into a letter of our alphabet: a letter which Nuala can lift so that she may learn to spell her own stories. The sight of Servants on their knees sanding the great board by hand, smoothing its edges with rough, then finer and finer sandpaper in steel holders, the back-and-forth scrapings hypnotizing in the breezy room.

I've asked the Carpenter-Servants to make extra letters. Enough to spell NUALA and TREE and TEA as many times as she likes without running out of the letters to do so.

I shield from Nuala my thoughts of the Servants painting letters on the Giant wooden tiles. I am especially careful to hide my thoughts of our young woman (to whom I have given the name Game-Servant) supervising the others in the creation of this wonder. I accompany her as she carries the small game board under her arm, unfolding it and shyly giving instruction to those painting the incorrect colour or not-quite-right words on a square.

The squeal and splinter of handsaws and rasps of sand-paper echo through the workshop. The edges of the great tiles are left rough so that Nuala may pick them up and hold them without frustration. They will not slip from her smooth fingers.

I walk among the toiling Servants, stepping over their paint cans and sawdust, my hands clasped behind my back, the ends of my long hair tickling my thumbs.

I am superfluous here. Game-Servant has the building process well in hand, but I enjoy watching her go about her duties: her gentle supervision. I will be able to tell Nuala about how the board was made, tell her stories of these Servants on their knees, sanding the board to a gleam, staining, and painting the long black lines that separate the squares.

My heart brightens as the game becomes itself, and escapes from the confines of the wooden slab in which it was hiding, waiting to be discovered by the careful hands working all around me.

I am buoyed by the idea of Nuala's thoughts focused and alert as I teach her the words she most longs to spell. As each new word enters her mind and her hands, she will have a new skill on which to set her thoughts: the next word. And the next and the next, until she will be ravenous to learn more. She will learn to spell out stories and dreams, delighting me with her pride in her new abilities. She will forget tea and trees and her longing for her own kind.

Perhaps I have been mistaken all along. Perhaps Nuala's reason for being is to learn to read and write, and this is the means by which she shall fulfill that purpose. This unfamiliar lightheartedness! And I am to teach her. My fellow Servants shall resent me no longer. This is her purpose; I'm convinced. And so it becomes mine.

Not all of my colleagues are pleased with my workshop presence in the small windows of time when Nuala is napping. Today, I overhear some of the Walking-Servants in a back corner of the alehouse discussing my relative lack of physical labour. If I could trade Nuala's dreams pounding into my abdomen for the hardest of work, I would do it, if only for a day. One day of blessed peace, of mental blankness. How little they understand that some days—as I look down at them from the height of her shoulder, rocking as her great legs lift and fall—I yearn for the quiet of their minds. I would lift her wrists over and over until my arms shook and my legs were rubber. I would lay my body down. Be the velvet cloak that covers the mud puddle through which she steps. For one day with a tranquil mind, I would be the ant who over and over carries many times his own weight to his Queen.

More Servants enter the tavern. If only these good fellows whining about me knew that their thoughtless words of envy floated to my ears. If they only knew with what madness my mind is always coloured, they would rejoice—rather than complain—that they could not understand what Nuala wants. That *they* are the blessed ones: privileged to be at her feet and not inside her head.

'I tell you,' one of the Kitchen-Servants says ordering their ale, 'Teacher-Servant has the easiest job in the Service. He rides on high, looking down on us moving her legs and arms, telling her stories, and have you seen the braids he puts in her hair?'

'That must be what she wants,' the other says.

'You have no more idea of what she *wants* than I have! We only know what Teacher-Servant stoops to *tell* us. I don't understand why we don't all know what she wants.' I hear a satisfied swallow as he drinks his ale. I grow light-headed on their loose talk. 'It's not right that only he knows these things.'

'You know the rules,' the quieter one says.

'You know what they're saying in the kitchen? When she learns how to make words, he won't be able to keep her thoughts from us if she wants to spell them out with her letters. No one can stop her telling us why she's alive, what her purpose is, and the thing I want to know most of all: why we serve her. She's going to tell us everything with that word game.'

'You can't read,' says his friend.

'That's beside the point!' the other shouts, and his tankard bangs on the table. '*You* can read, and you can read her words to me.'

'If I choose to. It will depend on how much ale you get me to keep your secret.'

'All you can drink, my friend. But it's nearly time for Her Majesty to wake up. We'd better get ready to serve the evening meal to the Walking- and Wrist-Servants once she is in bed, listening to the tales of our reclining, delicate Teacher-Servant. I don't remember him being this secret and aloof in the City of Servants. I don't know what it is about knowing Nuala's thoughts, but it's certainly made him get up on a pedestal the rest of us can't reach.'

'We are not Teacher-Servant,' the other says, 'and we don't know what goes on between them. I agree with you that he's changed. I don't understand what she could possibly have to say to him that's important enough for him to keep from us. But we knew when we joined the Service that only he would ever be able to speak with her. Until she chooses otherwise, we have to stay in the dark like everyone else.'

'It's not right, I say.' I hear their chair legs scraping across the wooden floor. 'I don't understand that rule and I don't agree...'

I lose the conversation as the two leave the alehouse. I am appalled and silenced. It had not crossed my mind that Nuala could use the word game to reveal her thoughts. How did this possibility not occur to me? What have I done? I am not to be trusted with anything, never mind the care of our Puppet Queen! My head in my hands does not take away the throbbing regret, the rush of cold fear that I have made the grandest mistake of my life.

Do *all* the Servants feel this way? Do they all resent and mock me? Surely not! Have they all imagined her spelling her thoughts on the word board? They truly seem to think that Nuala is wise and understands her place among us. That she will have something important, something I have been keeping from them, to tell once she decides to do so.

I laugh in a bitter spit of ale. Won't they be delighted when she spells HOT TEA over and over? What marvellous wisdom! And what of the endless, unvarying questions: Why this? Why that? Why, why? She'll run out of letters before these mean-spirited Servants learn the first thing about her tiny mind.

I turn my thoughts to Senior Iron-Servant. Of her regard and confidence, I am certain. But why did she not warn me that this might happen? She is wise, after all.

And to be held in such low regard by some of my number is a blow. I finish my drink, leave the alehouse, and make slow progress through the city toward the sleeping Giant, for I must be at her side when she awakens. Curse or gift, I must be at her side.

Her

new room is smaller, but closer to where Game-Servant now carries out her duties. For her, it is a short walk to oversee the creation of the word game, and if I am fortunate and Nuala lets me sleep, I am sometimes able to fall into step with her as we make our way toward our morning's work.

'Teacher-Servant,' she says. 'Nuala must be driving you mad as you no longer visit my old flat each week. How are you keeping?'

'It's very kind of you to ask about me, and I hope your mother is well.' I take her arm to steer her around a puddle in the street.

'Mother misses our weekly games, but we do find time every few days to sip tea and tell stories together. Now, tell me about Nuala.'

I squeeze her arm, its warmth easing the morning chill. 'Nuala's memory is an odd creature, and I'm slowly learning how it operates. When you became part of the Service, she all but forgot she had ever seen your flat. She loves you already, but I think her passionate affection for you in this new role will quickly grow. You may be overwhelmed by the force of her love once she sees you again.'

'I understand, Teacher-Servant. I'm prepared. I have a great capacity to love and be loved.' We pass the long low windows of the ironing room and call out our good mornings. I hear Senior Iron-Servant's cheerful call: 'Welcome, Game-Servant! May you find joy in the Service.'

'Thank you, Senior Iron-Servant. As I've already found great joy in Nuala's presence, I cannot but imagine that my joy will be trebled.'

As the women exchange these standard greetings, I take a moment to examine Game-Servant's profile. Her slim nose and long lashes would enthrall any Servant.

'While her dreams of you have diminished,' I tell her as we walk on, 'how I wish the same applied to her dreams of tea!

'We are exploring new streets now, and new wonders that she's not yet dreamed of. Now that we do not find ourselves almost daily at your lodgings, she has broadened her curiosity.

'She does love to venture to the graveyard at the edge of the city so that she may visit her trees, but I keep these visits to a minimum. You can't imagine the stern looks I received from the Iron-Servants the last time we returned, Nuala's dress coated in sap!

'There is one tree she has named *Family* and the few times we've visited, she whispers it the prettiest things you can imagine. Things I wish she still said to me. She loves them. I think all the love she once bore me has moved to her trees.' I find myself at the edge of tears.

'But I can tell you that the Wrist- and Walking-Servants have new life in their steps. They enjoyed bringing Nuala to your former home, but to take her somewhere different has given them new hope and new duties, negotiating unfamiliar streets and narrow alleyways. It tests their skills in ways they've not had to employ in weeks.'

We pass Servants of all kinds in the bright street, and each welcomes Game-Servant with the customary greeting.

'When we last approached the trees at the gates of the cemetery, Nuala spoke to them. *Hello, trees*, she said. *I am you and you are me.* At that moment, a small wind came up, their leaves and needles rustled, and she was overcome with joy. *Teacher-Servant!* she said. *Their thought-leaves are waving for me. They are thinking of me!* No longer does she constantly dream of other beings of wood, as she has now touched and stroked another of her kind, though unfeeling in the conventional sense. I suppose that should be of some comfort to me.'

'I'd have loved to have seen that moment,' she says.

We walk for a few paces in companionable silence.

'I've been meaning to tell you for the longest time, Teacher-Servant, that there is a tea shop a few miles beyond my old home. My shabby teacups are nothing compared to the beauties within that shop.'

She pauses to wave at one of her former colleagues: a Sewing-Servant beside whom she recently worked. She breaks from me and runs across the street. The two embrace as old friends do. He holds her at arm's length, studies her face. And I read the words, 'Are you happy?' on his lips. Her shining glance toward me is all the answer that's required, and I nod at the handsome young man.

She returns to me, looking over her shoulder and waving at the young man as he makes his way to the sewing workshop. 'My apologies. I have not seen him for some weeks. But I was telling you about the tea shop.

'On the days when I was not required in the sewing room, I disappeared into that shop for hours. If I was not at home when my mother arrived to play the word game, she would simply let herself in, put the kettle on, and read my books until I returned.

'But oh, the wonders in that tea shop, Teacher-Servant! I'm not surprised you haven't found it yet. It seems you hardly have any time to yourself.

'I wouldn't presume to tell you your duties, but I don't know how wise it would be to take Nuala there, as the shop is at ground level. It would be frustrating for her not to be able to see inside properly. But I wonder if you would let me choose a teacup and saucer she could keep in her room. It might help her to keep a glimmer of memory of the love she had for me before I became Game-Servant, when I still filled her thoughts, to my joy but to your detriment.'

'That is a thoughtful idea. Of course I give you full permission to choose a teacup you think Nuala will like. But do you have goods to barter? You've not been in the Service long enough to have acquired many wares to trade.'

'I have books, my friend. Hundreds of them. Poetry, mostly.'

'Poetry is all I read,' I burst in. 'How fortunate that we enjoy the same books. But I interrupted you—forgive me.'

She takes my arm. 'Quite all right, Teacher-Servant. It's delightful to find a fellow lover of books. For years, a friend gave me books, and I have two, sometimes three copies of the same volume.

'I'm sure the owner of the tea shop would consider a trade. I've noticed that though the shop has some books, they could use more. They have so many kinds of tea, you won't believe it. Rosehip with spices, black leaf tea of all kinds.'

'I would like to go there with you. Let us pick out a cup together. You know more about these things than I do, so I'll be happy to let you make the final choice.'

'That would be wonderful, Teacher-Servant. And you and I can share a pot of tea once we've chosen Nuala's gift.'

'Then we shall find time. It will have to be during Nuala's afternoon nap.' I cannot hide my sigh. 'I hear her waking now, and I must be at her side when Seeing-Servant opens her eyes or he shall be cross with me for arriving behind my time. I shall see you at the midday meal, and we can plan a trip to the tea shop together then.'

After

weeks of preparation and labour, the day of presentation has arrived. Today Nuala will receive the game, and her Servants scatter here and there, fussing with last-minute details and arrangements. The kitchen buzzes with activity. The sweet aroma of butter cake drifts into the square, and celebratory bottles of ale have been set to chill in tubs of ice.

Nuala is sitting in her afternoon chair, but she is not asleep. Her excitement is palpable, her earlobe hot to my touch. I sit on her shoulder and watch the scurrying Servants run to and fro, blowing to warm their fingers, preparing urns of coffee and setting out our traditional twice-baked sunflower bread. They pull the nearly cooked loaves from the deep ovens, sprinkle them with seeds, and put them back to bake until the sunflower seeds harden and release their scent, their aroma making my mouth water.

Below me, Servants hang colourful banners reading *Nuala Receives Her Gift Today!* around the square. Nuala's eyes are closed, and Head-Servant and I have placed a pretty sash over them. Her anticipation nearly knocks my skull from my head.

Game-Servant is resplendent in her pressed grey uniform with golden buttons, her hair left to blow free in the breeze. She is magnificent, and my heart surges when I consider that it was I who brought her into the Service.

All eyes but Nuala's are on the beautiful new Servant. She appears calm, and there is no doubt that Nuala will love the game, but this moment must be unnerving for her.

Under her supervision, ten Servants carry the great folding board and lay it at Nuala's feet. They lift the top half and it falls open with a *whomp* to reveal itself: hundreds of squares, some painted bright orange, and some the emerald of Nuala's eyes. Around the edges are squares the same deep greys of our tunics.

Excited Servants gather round the board. Two Washing-Servants and a Tea-Servant approach from the kitchen, wiping their hands on their aprons.

Senior Iron-Servant takes a tentative step toward the board. For weeks, the Servants have been walking, crawling, kneeling, and sitting on it, their tasks to sand or stain or polish or paint it.

Now, as it lies open in its finished state, Senior Iron-Servant looks as though she is about to tread on a sacred object. She glances at Game-Servant, and receiving a nod, she removes her shoes and steps onto the board. She slides her feet along as though she were skating. The other Servants laugh and remove their shoes.

Servants all over the board, laughing, sliding. Some kneel to read the words painted on the squares. *Wish a Wish. Hear a Story.*

'These squares must be where the tiles will go!' Tea-Servant exclaims, his pot of water forgotten on the stove. '*Tell a Dream. Tell a Secret.*' I shush him. Nuala must not hear of the game until she sees it!

Nuala can hear her Servants laughing. Her thoughts have been a steady muddle of excited bleats and questions, but I have blocked them as best I can to watch the dance of the small people below us. To see their joy, and to let my messy heart beat through this fresh and lively morning, the promise of a quieter Nuala once she sees her gift.

'Teacher-Servant! Never have I wanted my eyes to open as much as I do at this moment. When will I see my gift? I know you are astride my shoulder, even though you do not speak or think to me. I know your weight, your step, the scent of your hair. What is happening? I cannot hear you!'

'Do not fear, my love. I am here.' She relaxes at the sound of my voice.

Head-Servant and I take the great sheet of cloth from her eyes, and Seeing-Servant opens them for her. Servants move off the board so that Nuala may see it in its entirety, and they stand quiet to watch her take it in.

She has made herself tree, and sits straight and proud as she sees the gift. To my surprise, her mind is not the riot I expected.

'Do you see, little one?'

A moment passes. Then it begins. Her thoughts arrive mid-stream as if from a great distance, disjointed and half-uttered before they reach my brain. The words tumble over themselves in a babble of sound and cries of happiness piled atop one another in her head and mine. Thoughts and gasps in heaps and puddles. Minutes' worth of joy all arriving at once. My head splits with the weight of it. I cover my ears, but the gesture does nothing to calm the noise, and I am nearly thrown from her body.

The words slowly begin to untangle themselves to form sentences, cries, whispers, muted sobs. I lower my hands and beg Nuala to order her thoughts so that I can help her receive her gift. She sorts through her words and gives them to me.

'Teacher-Servant, it's the word game! Oh...' The jumble of words slows down. I understand with a knife-edged clarity that she'd been storing them up for this moment, hiding them from me, and when their weight became too much to bear, she released them to me, a fireball of sound and exclamations of love, for me, for the game, for her Servants. Never have I felt such pain, such exquisite penetration of desire, excitement, the leaping heart inside a body without one. I cradle my pounding head.

I have a moment of peace; the sight of two Iron-Servants dragging a great burgundy velvet bag distracts her. They drop it and it *click-click-click*s on the polished wood.

'I know what is in that bag!' she shoots to me. 'That is where the tiles are kept. The tiles with the letters upon them.'

'Little one, you are right.' The bag is so large that two Servants must hold it open while a young and lithe one crawls inside to retrieve a letter. He emerges holding a tile nearly too large for him to carry.

'I do not know this letter, Teacher-Servant, for it is not one of the letters that make up the word GIANT. I remember those letters. This one is different.'

'This is the letter L, Nuala. It is the first letter of *Love*, and of *Little*, and it is inside the word *Beloved* and inside the name *Nuala*.' I raise my voice and address the young man. 'The Servant has chosen his first letter well!' A cry of pleasure rises up from the Servants below.

'L,' Nuala repeats, holding the name of the letter in her mind.

'What must you do now, Nuala?'

'I must give the gift of my gaze to my Servants! I am pleased to do so.'

'I would like you to give your gaze to each Servant, for each one helped make this day so joyous for you. But first of all, I would like you to give your gaze to your new Game-Servant, for it is she who showed us how to build the game.'

'I will do so gladly, Teacher-Servant. She is beautiful. She is more beautiful than when she was my young woman in the small flat across the city. I do not yet have words to tell you of my love for her in this moment.'

Game-Servant walks to Nuala's side and kisses the back of her left hand as it hangs down over the arm of her sleeping chair. It is a long kiss. I feel the heat of Nuala's shoulder move through her crimson dress, and into my thighs.

Seeing-Servant moves his cables to pull Nuala's eyes from Game-Servant so that she may gaze on the others. She holds them on Game-Servant as long as she can, only looking away when Head-Servant lifts her face so that she has no choice but to cast her eyes about the square.

The bells clang in the courtyard amid great cries of celebration. Except for those of us in Nuala's direct service, today will be a day of leisure, cakes, ale, fresh bread. Dancing, music, and tea. I must work, but the kind Tea-Servant climbs the ladder up to Nuala's shoulder to pass me a canvas bag. Inside I find three bottles of ale, a slice of sweet sunflower bread, and a piece of butter cake, the aroma of which has been teasing me all morning.

Below us, the Servants have once again removed their shoes and are skating on the board, laughing, falling, and relishing the words. Those who cannot read sit next to those who can, and the spoken words start to sound like stories in the late morning sunshine.

The ale warms me and calms my mind. Perhaps this game will not be the disaster I imagine. Perhaps Nuala truly will spell HOT TEA until the Servants realize that I've not been hiding anything from them. I open a second bottle of ale, lean against Nuala's ear, and watch the dancing from my spot on high.

'**What** spectacle that was, Teacher-Servant!' Game-Servant has her arm through mine as we make our way along a winding street near the edge of the city. 'I was thrilled by her response to her Giant word game. I suppose it's pointless to teach her the actual rules of the game. It doesn't need to serve any purpose other than a teaching tool. Now the task falls to you to teach her to spell and read.'

'A task with which I hope you will assist me,' I say, suddenly bold. 'I need your help. I fear this whole endeavour has been a terrible mistake, Game-Servant. I fear to the point of paralysis that I've opened a gate that perhaps should have remained closed.

'If you will help me guide her learning, we may direct it in ways that do not compromise the stories I have told her. How I regret entrusting her with the details of my past, the stories I have told her of places that do not exist, knowing they could never leave her mind! Teaching Nuala is not part of your Service, but as the game's creator, you would be a great help as Nuala learns to use it. If this is her purpose, so be it, but I shudder at the thought of what she knows, what she might spell.'

We turn a corner to find a white stone storefront I have never seen before. 'I can see why you advised me not to bring Nuala here, Game-Servant. I do not believe this street is sufficiently wide for us to bring her safely through it, never mind the task of bending her low enough to see inside the tea shop she can never enter. Very wise on all counts that she should know nothing of this place. I'll do my best to shield my thoughts.'

We enter, and the shopkeeper greets Game-Servant with familiarity and warmth. We choose a teacup unlike the one Nuala broke. This one is white with many leaves, to remind her of her thought-leaves. The pot of rosehip tea we share is divine, and I feel Nuala's thoughts stirring toward it. I close my mind to her and embrace the moment.

'Do you think I hold Nuala's thoughts from you?'

Game-Servant blows across the tea. 'What I think doesn't matter, Teacher-Servant.'

'Oh, but it does, Game-Servant. I care more for your opinion than anyone's save Senior Iron-Servant.'

'All right,' she says and sets her tea down. 'I think that will be a moot point once she learns to use the word board to spell her thoughts and feelings. I think your fears are well-founded.'

'I was the last person to have thought of that possibility, when I should have been the first.' I am so distressed, I cannot meet her eye. 'How could I have made such a grievous error?'

'Don't blame yourself, Teacher-Servant. From what you've told me, you've had no peace since she saw my mother and me playing the word game. You can't have known what that sight would unleash in her mind. As I see it, you are doing your job in giving her what she desires. Perhaps, as you say, it's part of her purpose: to learn to read and write, and to share her thoughts with one and all.'

'I do not know, Game-Servant. I cannot know. Though I know her every thought. And until just recently, I believed I was the only one who ever would.' I take too quick a sip and burn my tongue.

As we walk back to Nuala's napping place, I tell my friend, 'We must each serve our role, Game-Servant. It is for me alone to determine Nuala's purpose, and until I know what that is, it is best that you not presume to guess at it.' My tone is sharper than I intend.

'Why would you feel the need to say that to me, Teacher-Servant? Every Servant knows that you are the authority where Nuala's thoughts and purpose are concerned. I will assist you in her education, however.'

I try to take her arm, but she moves away from me to step over some rubble, the satchel of tea and the cup she has chosen for Nuala tucked inside her elbow.

I have promised Nuala that if she settles down and goes to sleep quietly, tomorrow we will begin learning how to make words upon the game board. I have sworn that NUALA is the first word we will learn, and this knowledge has calmed her mind for the moment.

'The sooner I go to sleep, Teacher-Servant, the sooner I may awaken and begin learning with the word game! But please do tell me a story before the dreamtime. I remember Game-Servant's story about another Giant before me. Tell me a story of that Giant.'

Now that she will learn how to spell and to read, perhaps it is best that Nuala learns that all worlds hold ugly secrets. My every cell cries out against this, but the telling of myths of our city's past is not one of the Great Secrets. I must tell Nuala all she wishes to know.

'When I joined the Service, Nuala, a Mother-Giant was already a distant memory, and only in the minds of the very elderly among the city people. This may be difficult for you to understand as you will never grow old, but we who are made of flesh and blood age. We forget things about the Giant we may have seen years and years ago, and our bodies grow physically weak along with our minds. It is not as simple as oiling our joints to keep them supple.

'These elders remember a towering presence, but they cannot tell me what she looked like. Was her hair blonde like yours? Let us have a story together, and we will find out.'

'Yes, Teacher-Servant,' my beloved says, so close to sleep that I doubt she will hear the story through to its conclusion. I do not know the conclusion myself.

I stretch out next to Nuala's left ear, covering myself with a corner of her great blanket. I lay my lips against her earlobe, cool now to my touch.

'A Mother-Giant returned from a great journey across the sea. She came to the city and walked both its wide and narrow streets. She was dressed in a long gown of gossamer and flowers. The wind sang around the tall buildings and danced with the Mother-Giant's hair. She lifted her eyes to the skyline and looked for the little one she had longed for while she was adventuring in the Land of Giants. There were Daughter-Giants in that Land, but none belonged to her.

'The Mother-Giant sang through the city as she walked, her Servants lifting her, helping her move and walk and dream and seek.'

A sleepy voice: 'The Mother-Giant had Servants too?'

'Yes, little one. Many Servants, just as you do. She sang the song that only her little one could hear. The young Giant was playing with her word game when she heard the Mother-Giant's beckoning trills. She stopped playing, and listened. The sounds came from over the tops of the buildings. The little one had never known a Mother-Giant, and so she did not know how she would look or smell or sound. But the song she heard was so sweet, like honey running over glass, that the little one knew it could only be for her.'

Nuala's breathing steadies and deepens, and I lift the corner of the blanket. 'Teacher-Servant. I am not asleep. Please finish the story.' I tuck myself against her again, so tired I am in danger of falling asleep beside her. I busy myself with a loose braid to keep myself from drifting off.

'When the young one saw the Mother-Giant striding toward her, she let go of the letter tiles she was holding, and her Servants helped her stand. The Mother-Giant walked until she could reach out and place her hand on the head of the young Giant. The little one closed her eyes with the pleasure the touch brought her. The Engine holding the young Giant lifted her from the ground so that she could look into the eyes of the Mother-Giant. All the Servants helped the two Giants embrace for the first time in many years.

'The Mother-Giant touched the young Giant's cheek and stroked her hair. She held the young Giant to her oaken breast. The Mother-Giant's Wrist-Servants helped her wrap her great arms around the wooden girl. They stayed in the embrace for a long time, until their Servants became too tired to hold them. The Giants never wanted to move again, but if Giants do not move, they cease to love. So at last they were forced to part, and the sight of wires replaced the sight of one another.'

I feel Nuala drifting into sleep. Whatever happens in her dreams tonight, I have brought it upon myself. Just as she rides the very edge of consciousness, I whisper, 'This will never happen, little one. The last Great Giant is lost. She will never return for you.'

Nuala

wakens, thoughts full of mothers. She thinks me, 'Teacher-Servant, I would know the Mother-Giant by the song she sings. If she sang the song meant for me, I would hear her, and I would answer. I did not tell you each of the many times I wished to see the Mother-Giant as I feared it would make you sad. You are such a tiny thing, so easily hurt. So tiny when you walk on my lap, or brush my hair from my face.'

'Tiny things can hold a lot of pain, Nuala,' I think her from my lodgings. 'You mustn't hide from me thoughts that you worry will make me sad. Some thoughts will, but others will bring me joy. Have you been hiding your thoughts from me for some time?'

'No. It is only now that I find I have done it. You must think me unforgivably naughty.'

'I do not, my love.' I wash my face and tie my hair back. 'But I'll tell you again that you should not keep your thoughts from me. I am your Teacher-Servant. My work is made more difficult if I do not know what troubles you. If I do not know what your questions are, I cannot answer them.'

I make my way to where she lies awake.

'I have so many questions, Teacher-Servant. Why is it you who holds me at night and tells me stories? My arms ache for the embrace of something larger than me. There is so little big enough for me to curl into. Only my trees, and they cannot hold me, for they do not have arms. When shall I see them again?

117

'I remember, and yet I do not. Perhaps it is your stories that make me feel I remember a Mother-Giant. Perhaps I have a story-memory of long arms of wood and metal. The bolts and rivets of a Giant's arms. The rattle and shiver of my thought-leaves moving with hers. Other little Giants must feel this warmth. Why not I?'

I arrive at her side, climb the ladder to her cheek, and open her left eye for her.

'I do not have these answers, little one. I have only stories. I am sorry if they are not enough.'

'If you do not have the answers, then there is no hope of my ever knowing. For who else would know?'

'No one, my love. For now, is it not enough that you love and are loved? That you have your Servants, your trees, the word game, the stories I tell you, our wanderings?'

'These shall have to be enough, Teacher-Servant, for I fear there is nothing else.'

Nuala's

education in the word game is swift. Her mind, at its most passionate in search of knowledge, terrifies me. She stares with penetrating intensity at the letters on the word board. Sometimes I move the letters for her, but she prefers to move them herself, with the help of her Wrist-Servants.

I am silenced by her new voice. She can spell simple sentences now. NUALA WANTS TEA. Tea-Servant asks me if he may bring her some, but I remind them both that she cannot drink it. Her mouth is forever sealed. The teacup Game-Servant has given her is the closest she will come to experiencing tea. I am still the arbiter in all matters concerning Nuala's care.

The

Engine lifts Nuala and sets her down on the edge of the bed. The Clothing-Servants have kept their hands in their tunic pockets so they will not be chilly on Nuala's bare wood. Head-Servant and a Wrist-Servant undo the clamps that hold her to the Engine, and it extracts its snake-arm from her spine. Soon, all the wires are removed except for the one attached to the top of her head. Everything is clear to her in this deepening time of shadow and setting sun.

I watch as the Clothing-Servants unbutton the crimson dress and slip it from her shoulders. They pull the fabric over her wrists and remove the garment. She sits naked for a time, her polished chest of rosewood, her kneecaps and hips cool in the evening air.

I turn my eyes away. She is my beloved. I will not gaze upon her nakedness.

They pull her pink nightdress over her hands, her elbows. It is now that I join the team preparing her for bed. Only I may reach in and tug her hair from inside her nightgown and lay it over her shoulders. Smooth it before her head is lowered.

When her head is on her Giant pillow, Head-Servant will release the last brass clasp and Nuala will be free. Free to sleep and free to dream. Free to turn my dreams wild, to cage me in the mental prison of her word game and her love for Game-Servant. I wish I were dead.

'What does it mean to be *dead*, Teacher-Servant?'

Every drop of my blood congeals, each one rescinding its promise to keep me alive.

I collect myself. 'You are fortunate in that you will never know, my child. Imagine a place where no one loves you. Imagine a place so much changed when you return after a long absence that you do not recognize it. A place where people surround you, and yet you are utterly alone. Where the wind blows through the buildings and streets and false giants you once loved. That is what death is like. A watching, an aloneness, a fear, a loss of purpose.'

The Waking-Servants pull the citizens' long-ago quilt over her frame, and I climb onto the pillow next to her head.

'Teacher-Servant, I know you hide a story from me. I hear it in your thoughts and in words like *dead*. It frightens you, and yet you keep it to yourself. Is not your purpose to tell me all that I wish?'

'And is not *your* purpose to do as I bid, knowing that I know what is best for you?'

'You cannot hide the story from me forever, Teacher-Servant. I see bits of it in the corners of your mind. When I am learning to spell with Game-Servant, she sometimes talks of you. She says that...'

'Game-Servant!' I snap. 'Can you not utter one sentence without her name in it? Can you not have a single thought that is of me and not always, always of her?'

She is silent for a long moment. 'Teacher-Servant, I believe I speak many sentences without using Game-Servant's name. But it is she who brought me the word game, she who teaches me, she who loves me.'

'*She* who loves you. Listen to yourself. All right, Nuala. If you want my hidden story, you shall have it.'

I calm myself and in so doing, I calm her as well. We take deep breaths together, each silently vowing to the other through the warmth of our bodies that this will be the last time we quarrel. The promise is empty, but we obey the ritual.

'You must not blame me if the story frightens you. Were you not so demanding, I should have held this story forever. For *love* of you.

'In another world, far away from here, and far from the Land of Giants and the City of Servants, there is a place where the Giants have four arms and seven fingers on each hand. These Giants are hunters and they seek out the tiny people in their cities for food. The small people have taken to underground tunnels they have constructed so that they may hide from the Hunter-Giants. These Giants roam freely, treading upon and killing any small people who are unfortunate enough to be on the surface looking for food of their own.

'The lairs of the tiny people are safe from the Hunter-Giants, as they are too large to fit inside the holes the small people have tunnelled into the earth. But the Hunter-Giants are not tied to Engines, and may jump upon the ground above the heads of the small people—for the Hunter-Giants can smell them hiding below—until the earth caves in and crushes the people beneath it. The Hunter-Giants then turn scavenger.'

As I tell my story, I close Nuala's eyes, my hands at their most tender. My feet sink into the pillow as I walk to her left eye. She wills it to stay open, but she must yield to my touch. I climb onto her face and gentle down the reluctant lid. Run my hand down the bridge of her nose in the gesture she finds so calming. She may appear to be sound asleep, but she will be wide awake in terror of the night-time Hunter-Giants, who could come to her city at any moment. As she lies awake, willing Game-Servant to come and save her, I may find a moment's peace and rest. It is time she learned of the horrors in the world. It is time she grew up.

In my room, I am on the cusp of sleep when her voice comes to me, groggy and frightened: 'Is the world wicked and full of secrets and Hunter-Giants, Teacher-Servant?'

'The world is not wicked, my love. But the world contains wickedness. As all worlds do.' I lose myself to the blessed unconscious, but—just as I deserve—I am torn limb from limb as the Hunter-Giants of Nuala's dream splash me across their land. She dreams that she is helpless and untied on the ground, the Engine nowhere to be seen. Bits of my body splatter her limbs and cheeks.

My Nuala is learning so fast, her brain is turning and turning, and all she wants is words, words, more words. I miss her asking me to crawl up into her lap, to lay the ladder against her hip, and climb to her shoulder. All she desires is spelling.

I've not heard the mumblings of the disgruntled Kitchen-Servants since Nuala has begun to share her thoughts on the game board. NUALA LOVES GAME SERVANT. MOTHER GIANT. BELOVED.

There, envious Servants. There is her *wisdom*! NUALA LOVES GAME SERVANT. Your wishes have been granted. You now know all that is in her head.

I have given up trying to read in the afternoons during her naps, and have taken to sitting in the tavern near the fire while she dreams. The ale is bitter and refreshing, and I can take off my straitjacket of a tunic. Today I share a pitcher of ale with Senior Iron-Servant.

'We are still being kept, and kept well,' she says. 'But for what? You, Head-Servant, Seeing-Servant, Game-Servant, and the Wrist-Servants are all guaranteed employment indefinitely, but what is to become of the rest of us? The Walking-Servants haven't worked in weeks, and they are starting to resent their temporary duties in the kitchen. I am as well, if you must know. If Nuala no longer gets dirty and wrinkled, what need of me and my team of Iron-Servants to clean and press her garments? We all spend more time in this alehouse than we should, and we're none of us happy. I do detest trying to get sap out of her dress, but if it would give us all something to do, I beg you to take her to see her trees if that is what she desires. Do not give a thought to our cleaning duties afterward.'

She pauses, then adds, 'I wish the word game had never been built, Teacher-Servant.'

I have no answers for her. 'She's not mentioned her trees in weeks,' I sigh. 'You mustn't blame *me*, my friend. You know as well as anyone that aside from the Great Secrets, Nuala is to be granted what she desires. You must trust that I know what she most covets. You can't imagine that *I* dreamed up a giant word game, can you? I feel such a stab of regret that I was not able to prevent her from seeing that word game in the first place. Prevent her from seeing Game-Servant. Prevent *me* from seeing Game-Servant.

'Earlier, I watched Nuala spell out MY BELOVED. A Walking-Servant asked, *Who is that?* I was mortified to the roots of my hair. What business was it of hers?

'*It is what we sometimes call one another,* I had to explain. The Servant was shocked, and asked me if that was appropriate. Another was charmed by my *whimsy.* Must I now share these things with anyone who asks? What is the point of having a station that allows me to be the only one to truly know the secrets of Nuala's thoughts if anyone can now discover them, banal as they are?'

Relief rolls through me. I have not spoken aloud of these things to anyone. Senior Iron-Servant pours us both more ale.

'Nuala used to spell TEACHER SERVANT more than any other words, but no longer. Sometimes Game-Servant will join us in the lessons so that she can inspect the word game. To see that none of the letters are lost, that the board remains shiny and sanded. Game-Servant speaks words to Nuala that would turn any Giant's head. Someone able to supervise the creation of a wonder like the word game has mouthfuls of pretty words. *You look radiant, Nuala,* she said yesterday. And then I had to teach her how to spell RADIANT! She lives to please Game-Servant, it seems.'

'Perhaps,' my friend says. 'But it is you she loves.'

'I am no longer sure. I once thought Game-Servant and I might be friends. She seemed to enjoy spending time with me. She kissed me once. But now I can sense haughtiness and self-satisfaction rising from her, she of the grey tunic and the hot tea and the eyes as violet as the letter bag that holds the blessed, wretched letters I have come to hate. Neither of them seems to have a thought left for me these days.'

'Can Nuala hear you now?'

'I don't think so. I've nearly perfected the task of shielding my mind from hers. What was I thinking, offering Game-Servant employment?'

'You were doing your job, Teacher-Servant. There are those who fault you for that. I do not, even if this costs me my position, but that's because I love you and have known you since you were a boy. Others do not feel the same.'

'I'm aware of their censure,' I say, looking down at my trembling hands.

'I worry most for you, Teacher-Servant. Do I need to remind you of the lore of the first Teacher-Servants, of what happened to them?'

'My dear friend! Do you imagine that I have not been to the archives and tortured myself, poring over the dusty books, looking for the stories of the first Teacher-Servants who went mad with grief, writhing half-clothed, running through endless and unsearchable woods calling to the Giants who broke free and abandoned them? Do you imagine I have thought of anything else? Spare me your concern if you please, your misplaced and invasive...'

The tears spill before I can stop them. She stands and moves to my side of the table, wraps her arms around me and places her cheek on the top of my head until I am quiet, spent.

I seethe, spelling the word RADIANT over and over until I run out of the letters I need to do so. Game-Servant looks on. Nuala's cheeks glow, and even the wind conspires to thwart my efforts to banish Game-Servant from Nuala's every thought. It whips Game-Servant's hair around her pretty mouth. I watch her strong hands pushing it back from her face, wish for the days when it was she and I sipping hot spicy tea, this puppet the furthest thought from our heads.

'Beloved,' I say, looking straight into Game-Servant's eyes. Head-Servant turns Nuala's face toward me. 'We must finish your lessons. We cannot learn only RADIANT today.'

She moves her eyes down without the help of Seeing-Servant. I freeze at the wilfulness of her act.

'Now, now. Do not cast your eyes down. Was it not you who so badly wanted the word game? You who wanted so much to learn how to spell the words of your desires? Of what use is it to spell RADIANT over and over again? There are so many other words to learn, my love.'

She is forced to see me, to look at me. I place myself in her direct line of vision. She must see me. Her beloved. Her Teacher-Servant.

'If you do not listen, little one, I shall have to send Game-Servant away. When did you become so naughty and contrary?'

When I turn back to look her way, Game-Servant is gone.

TREE SPEAK.

We have not visited the cemetery in months, and now that the leaves are well into their golden and brittle journey toward death in the low autumn sun, they are what she misses most, what she needs most. They must miss her in return.

The Servants are overjoyed. Something to do! The Iron-Servants return to their tasks of airing and ironing Nuala's dress and socks. They assure me they will not mind removing sap from the fabric. The Wrist-Servants—who have been in a near-stupor of boredom, helping Nuala lift letters over and over, spelling the same words in a mind-numbing repetitive motion—now oil and check the joints and cables to her rusting shoulders, her creaking elbows.

Excitement sings in the autumn city. The morning is a flurry of activity: Kitchen-Servants pack lunches of cake and ale, twice-baked bread normally reserved for special occasions. I make the case that Nuala's desire to walk is a special occasion, and the Servants set to, wrapping thick-sliced honey bread in parchment for the long day ahead.

We set out in the early morning. Nuala's mind is quiet today, to my surprise. 'What are you thinking about, my love?' I ask her, my thighs comfortable on her shoulder, my hands in her hair as I hold myself steady.

'Can you not tell?'

'This morning, no; I cannot.'

'It is no matter. I am thinking about what I shall say to the trees when I see them again. I wonder what they will say in return.'

'That is a lovely thought, Nuala. Why not open your mind to me now? I shall help you think of the perfect things to say to your friends, the trees.'

'They are not my friends, Teacher-Servant. They are who I am. They are all the family I shall ever have.'

My throat closes. 'Nuala, you cannot think such a thing! Why, I am your family. And what of Senior Iron-Servant? Oh, Nuala, what of Game-Servant? Surely you think of *her* as family.'

'I do not, Teacher-Servant. I may love you all, but love and family are not the same. Because you are not Giants and because you are not made of wood, we cannot be family.'

The remainder of the long walk to the cemetery, she is silent. I open my mind to her, calling up memories of when she first awoke, of the love we felt for one another. I revisit my favourite memory of the two of us: the day I leaned my body into her lips while removing her rain hat, and she asked me, 'Is this what Giant love feels like?' Never have I had such joy as I did in that moment. I allow this bliss to roll over me, to penetrate and cleanse me, head to toe. The memory forces a groan from my throat: the sure and certain knowledge that in that moment, I was she, and she was me, and in our eyes the love of centuries passed under a purple rain hat.

If she hears my thoughts, she does not respond. I feel nothing but the movement of her legs under me, the coolness of her earlobe against my palm. If she shares this memory, she does not allow me to feel it.

I have never been so alone in my life.

'Here we are, Nuala!' I say, my voice full with cheer for the benefit of the Servants. Her earlobe warms at the sight of the tall spruce and pine rising before her as we approach.

'Servants! Please bring Nuala close to the trees. We will allow her as much private time as she wishes with them while we take our refreshments at some distance.' Only the Engine will remain to hold Nuala in the embrace of her beloved trees.

'Teacher-Servant,' she says, her voice that of my little one again. 'Please have the Servants move me so that my face is touching the tallest tree. The one I call Family.' As though I hadn't heard her perfectly well the first time.

I call down and my Queen is manoeuvred to stand next to the tallest moss-covered pine. The Servants gently lever down her arms. Around us, scattered poplars sway, the flashy yellow fires of their last leaves holding on until the end.

Seeing-Servant and Head-Servant clamber down from the Engine, I climb down the rope ladder to jump to the ground, and we remove ourselves to a respectful distance so that Nuala may speak privately with her trees, but where I am close enough to observe and be at her side quickly in case she calls to me.

'Teacher-Servant,' a Wrist-Servant asks, 'what is it she wants with the trees? Everyone knows that even if she speaks to them, they might not speak back.'

I swallow a bite of honey bread not noticing its sweetness, so muddled and sad are my thoughts.

'She believes the trees speak to her in the rustle of their leaves and needles and branches. I have not dissuaded her, and in her child-mind, it gives her comfort.' I take a long pull from a bottle of cold ale. 'Imagine if you were the only one of your kind in the Great City. You would be lonely for others like yourself, even if they could not speak to you.'

Hours

pass. She stands unmoving. The Servants and I wrap ourselves in blankets, tell stories, drink ale, and recline on our backs in the long, low sunlight.

She does not call me.

The trees sway around her, branches brushing her arms and face, a tangle of moss caresses her hair in the way only I am permitted to do.

I catch snippets of the stories she tells them. 'And it was the word game, dear trees, the word game!...Engine...Freedom.'

If the trees respond to her, I cannot read their thoughts. She does not call to me. The sun makes its way behind the tallest of the poplars. I call, 'Nuala. It is time to go home now, before it gets dark.'

'I do not wish to leave here, Teacher-Servant. I do not wish to leave my family.'

'You know that is impossible, my beloved.'

'Stop calling me that! If I were truly your beloved, you would grant me what I wish.'

The others remain at the distance I ask them to keep. I stand at her feet, wrapped around the solid bulk of her ankle. Around the sturdy oak I have taught her to become, my tears sink into the ground at her exposed roots.

I am overcome by a wild desire to please her. The words spill from me.

'Nuala: if you will behave and come home cheerfully, you shall have hot tea. Remember the lovely teacup Game-Servant traded her precious books to obtain for you? Tonight, if you listen and do as I bid, I will find a way to serve you hot tea from that cup.'

A long pause. 'I shall do as you say, Teacher-Servant.' Then a longer sob of a farewell to her trees. At last, I climb her, and we wend our way home.

'You

have promised me that I shall drink hot tea tonight, Teacher-Servant,' Nuala says as I ride her shoulder. She has repeated the sentiment a dozen times since we began our walk home. I have finished three bottles of ale while upon her shoulder, and there are two more in my pocket; but sometimes, there is not enough ale in the world.

'And so you shall, little one, but let us get you home first. You must remember, though, that I do not believe that you will be able to taste the tea. It will not stay inside you. It will not warm you as it warms your Servants of flesh and blood.'

The movement of her shoulder is unsettling my guts. I should regret the ale, but I do not. It is all that holds me steady tonight.

'Yes, yes, you have told me all this,' she says. 'But I can smell, Teacher-Servant. I can feel love and fear. Why may I not taste? I must ask myself, Teacher-Servant, why this is the one wish you have never granted me. You had the Servants build me the word game. You take me to see my trees when I desire it, though you fight me, and I desire it more often than you allow it. Why the tea? Why do you withhold it from me when you know it is what I most desire? Is it because tea is what you share with Game-Servant?'

Even though it is a warm fall evening, I grow cold.

'Oh, do not think I cannot see your thoughts of her,' she says, 'as you sit in the teahouse I shall never see, sipping and looking at one another, touching her face as you touch mine. For I know these things. You do your best to conceal these thoughts, Teacher-Servant, but my mind is growing, and I am able to reach into yours when you do not know I am there. Are you hiding the magic secret of tea from me? I demand to know the why of it.'

'My love,' I say, my voice measured and my thoughts closed. 'I hide nothing. I have been more honest with you about the taste of tea than I have been about almost everything else. Though you may see and hear, feel, touch, and smell, you cannot taste. You have no tongue. We know this from our work with the false Giants. Perhaps you once did, but you know that your mouth is closed forever.'

As we approach her sleeping place, I call out to all. 'Thank you for your service today. It is such a mild evening, dear Servants. Would you be so kind as to place Nuala in her afternoon sleeping chair for the night so that she may see the vivid stars before she sleeps? I will stay with her, I will close her eyes, and I will ensure that she is not frightened should she awaken, and not know where she is.'

She is lifted, lowered, unhooked; the Waking-Servants have covered her and cooed her a lullaby. I have asked Seeing-Servant to leave her eyes open, the better to see the diamonds of night above our heads. Then I ask that she and I be left alone and unobserved.

I settle the long ladder in her lap and rest it against her chin. Up against her mouth, I find exactly what I'd expected. There is no gap between her upper and lower lip. I only need an inch in which to pour the tea, but I have not even that.

'Nuala, my love. I cannot help you sip hot tea unless I open your mouth a tiny bit. My fear is that this will cause you pain.'

'Nothing pains me as much as you do, Teacher-Servant. Your cruel words, your terrible stories, your hidden cups of tea with Game-Servant, your pulling me away from my tree-family, bribing me with empty promises. No amount of pain you may cause me now could equal all of that.'

135

My guts fall to ashes and I lean against her closed mouth, hoping for the wooden kiss of long ago, the kiss that showed me she loved me above all.

I shall never have that kiss again. Her lip is cold against my torso. 'I will be back with the necessary tools,' I tell her. Her eyes and mind are open, but she does not answer me.

I climb down and enter the blacksmith's shop. Near the fire, I find a blackened iron crow. I climb back up Nuala and show her the tool. 'I do not know what pain this will cause you, my beloved.'

'Do it,' she says, her resolve sharp, her thoughts measured. I lean my body against her chin and place the iron crow between her lips. My movements are as tender as I can make them under these violent circumstances. I lever the crow an inch or two, and am startled by the scream of the nails at either side of her lips as they give way. A thousand years of red dust blows into my face as the nails nearest her mouth disintegrate.

Nuala's mind is a blast of rust and pain. I stop and remove the crow. I have hurt my beloved. She lies, mouth open an inch, red scars where the nails had held it closed for so many years.

'My little one. My Nuala! You cannot know my regret at this pain I have caused you.' I am paralyzed with this wanting to go back, just five moments, to where I had not tried to fulfill her most ardent wish.

'I feel nothing, Teacher-Servant.' I am slapped by the knowledge that this is not the first time she has lied to me.

'I will make the tea as I like to drink it: hot and sweet with thick milk to make it as smooth and delicious for you as I can. Lie here. Do not be afraid while I am gone.'

'Nothing holds the power to cause me fear any more, Teacher-Servant. I shall wait for your return.'

The kitchen is dark, but I know where the tea things are. I set the small kettle to boil and walk to Nuala's bedroom, where I find the teacup Game-Servant gifted her, next to the pottery bowl with the old, dusty lock of my hair that has lain here for a year. In the kitchen, I find the tin of loose black tea, and search through the drawers until I locate the tea strainer. Under the cupboard is a cream teapot hidden inside a red cozy. I find a milk jug in the pantry and sugar in a jar near the windows.

I steep the tea and sweeten it the way I like it. I place the cup into my tunic pocket and make my way back to where Nuala lays, quiet and awake. It's awkward and precarious climbing the ladder with the full teapot in my hand, but I reach her chin without spilling.

'My beloved, I have made you hot tea. Are you ready to drink it for the first time?' My Nuala of the past would be beyond speech and thought in her anticipation of this most desired of delicacies. My Nuala now thinks me nothing more than a dispassionate 'Yes.'

I pour the tea into the cup and hold it to her wooden lips, then tilt it. The liquid spills through the coiled metal of her throat, dribbles down her back and pools on the ground below her chair in a long snake of fragrant brown liquid. Her hair is sticky with it. I empty the cup into her, and every drop spills from her tongueless mouth, from her untasting mouth. Exactly as I told her it would. Along with it drains the last of her belief in me, the last of her faith in my teachings and love.

'I taste nothing, Servant,' she thinks me. Servant! Am I reduced to this?

'I'll kindly remind you to use my full name, Nuala.'

'I cannot taste the tea. You must have made it so.'

'Nuala!' I drop the teapot to the ground. It shatters, sending liquid and shards of pottery flying. 'I told you that the taste of tea is something you might not experience. I never lied to you about this.'

'But you have lied to me about so many other things. Please leave me, Servant, and let me sleep.'

'May I close your eyes for you?' I ask, in a last desperate attempt at intimacy with her, my beloved, my Nuala.

'You know I can do that on my own. You have always known.'

I drag myself back to my room, sick with longing and guilt.

Nuala

says she has had a terrifying dream she wants to tell me. I ask her leave to eat breakfast first. She woke me so early today, I did not have time to eat the morning meal the Kitchen-Servants prepared for me.

In the dining hall, the Kitchen-Servants dish out trays laden with steaming oatmeal, sunflower bread, eggs, and buttermilk biscuits. Urns of coffee stand on long tables, along with hot water for tea. I sip with immense pleasure and concentrate on the taste and warmth of this tea, until I am sure that Nuala is mad with the knowledge that she will never taste it.

If the Tea-Servant notices the missing teapot, he says nothing.

I go to her. She is awake, but her eyes are closed. The pottery has been cleaned up. I can only guess that Senior Iron-Servant arose early to save me from shame, to save me explaining its shattered pieces.

'I must tell you my dream,' she whispers as I stand before her, sipping my tea with the most pleasure I can muster.

'Why don't you spell it out on your word board for everyone to read?'

She is calm. 'Teacher-Servant, I ask for your body upon my shoulder.'

What is this? For a moment, I am buoyed by her request, her use of my full name. I climb up and am cradled at once in the familiar tender soft of her, her sheltering hair and warm earlobe.

'I ask for your head against my ear.' I comply, and my body sags against her, my love for her as sharp as the day she first awakened to see my face looking down upon her: my Puppet Queen, my Nuala.

'Nuala, I have behaved terribly toward you.'

'Hush now, Teacher-Servant, and let me tell you my dream, so that you may help me understand what it means, and help me not to be frightened.'

I know all her dreams. She cannot surprise me.

'In the dream, I saw a small wooden girl far across the sea,' she tells me. 'The girl I saw loved her Teacher-Servant, and he her. He was her storyteller, just as you are mine, and I am yours. The brusher of hair and the whisperer of secrets.'

I do not recognize this dream. For the sharpest of moments, hope shoots through me. Perhaps she has dreams that I do not share! I relax further into the oak of her shoulder.

I curl my legs up under me, her hair my blanket, my hands at her warm earlobe.

'The tiny Giant of my dream found herself in a forest she desired to explore. She asked her Teacher-Servant if she could lie among her great trees, and think about the mother she never knew, and the other Giants she hoped to meet one day. She desired to speak to the trees the way I speak to my own.

'As the small Giant lay in the woods, her Servants all having left her so she could speak her private tree-words, she drifted into sleep. Her Servants were alarmed some time later to see smoke rising into the sky from the place where she lay asleep. They hastened into the forest to find her burning. How terrified she must have been! How careless of her Servants not to leave one of their number to watch over her. How careless of her Teacher-Servant! They tried to douse the flames, but it was too late. She burned well into the night, lighting up the woods with the terrible glow of her fire.

'By morning, the beautiful little Giant was nothing more than a framework of metal and charred wood. Her body lay in ruins, smoke still rising from the black heap of ashes that was once her face, her child-wrists, her long yellow hair. The strong, sturdy oak inside her was charred and ruined by fire, all the leaves of her mind curled in on themselves, no longer able to think thoughts of love, one hand smouldering on the ground next to her.

'In my dream, the Teacher-Servant found himself wandering place to place, the smell of burnt hair stuck in his nostrils. His heart torn from his flesh-and-blood chest, he found himself on ships tossed by sea. He wandered through deserts and forests, looking for Giants and listening for rumours of Giants. In each city, there was always someone who had heard of them. But he never found them because he knew—as you and I know, Teacher-Servant—that there is no Land of Giants. It was then that I awoke.'

I take her in my arms the best I can. My tears soak into the fabric at her shoulder, my own outstretched arms. I bury my face in her hair and weep until I can weep no more. I lose my hands in her hair, tucking, holding, until I hide myself completely inside her hair, my wet face against the dry cold metal of her throat.

I hear one thought: 'This was not my dream, Teacher-Servant. I have merely told you a story.' Her earlobe is cold, her mind closed.

I climb down from her, numb, wounded in ways I did not know it was possible for a flesh-and-blood body to be wounded. Her duplicity mirrors my own. Surpasses it. Is it this for which I have groomed her? I am a failure. How I regret my subtle cruelties toward her, my jealousy, my flaunting of things she could never have. How dare I pour tea down her throat, knowing it had nowhere to settle, that her lack of a tongue would ensure she could never taste it. I knew all this, and yet I carried out the ritual in loving fashion, even as I knew it would not be as she desired.

Shaken, I walk to the tavern to drown my emotions in alcohol. Today there shall be no pretence about hiding my thoughts from her. It is clear I can no longer do that. She knows my every thought, my every desire, my every glaring flaw.

I take my usual table in the corner, unseen but within earshot of most of the tables in the larger room. I fill my mouth with ale, and as I lift the second of what I hope will be many drinks this afternoon while Nuala naps, I look up to see the face of Game-Servant. My heart leaps within me, and I rise and pull out a chair for her. I signal for more ale.

'I thought I might find you here,' she says, as though all that has passed between us were nothing more than a small professional disagreement.

'Please sit down, Game-Servant. Your company will be most agreeable to me.'

'I'm not certain you're telling me the truth, but I would like to speak with you.' She sits and pours herself a tall glass of ale.

'We're at odds and I am unhappy about it. When you asked me to join the Service, I didn't imagine that you would ever feel resentment toward me. You already knew Nuala's emotions concerning me, and I assumed that you were content to accept them. But you became envious, almost belligerent. I should have taken you seriously when you told me last spring that Nuala's feelings for me were making you jealous. But back then, the sunshine, the breeze, you on her shoulder, the magic of Nuala herself—all these made me unaware of anything hiding beneath your surface.'

'I was joking at that time, Game-Servant. Or more accurately, I thought I was. I do not know if we can reconcile after all that has happened between us, and now that you are clearly more in Nuala's favour than I ever was. This is not your fault, and yet, I cannot blame Nuala. She is a child. So who is to blame?'

'I do not know.' We drink in silence for a moment. 'But I do know that I miss you.'

She touches my hand across the table, then pulls back, sharply. She sits upright, eyes widening, an electricity spilling from her and lodging in my abdomen. 'I felt her awaken from her nap just now.'

I am on my feet in an instant. 'How can *you* feel her? I felt nothing!'

'I don't know, Teacher-Servant! What I know is that she is awake. And she is calling for me.'

'You shall not go to her without me. *I* am Teacher-Servant. You are merely Game-Servant.'

We leave the tavern and hurry to Nuala's napping chair. She is unhooked and reclining, but her eyes are open, moving on their own. The Servants rush toward her, assuming their assigned places. She is rigged, the Engine stabs her in her spine, she is raised to stand. I wait on the ground before her, my grey slippers in my hand, ready to crawl up her body at her command. Game-Servant stands next to me. I shake her hand from my arm.

Nuala's eyes light upon me. Servants and citizens alike watch me, rumpled and exhausted, slightly drunk.

From Nuala's eyes, there is a great pull on my sternum. A Giant hand of wood and metal reaches through my chest, parts my ribs, squeezes my heart, and I explode in a paroxysm of such loss, I crash to my knees before her. My Puppet Queen. Our eyes are locked, but there is nothing in hers. Her emeralds dull to a deep viridian. I read nothing. I see nothing.

'Nuala! I cannot hear you! What are you saying?'

Nothing. I hold my head in my hands for fear it will fall off if I do not support it. I am hollowed out. Ashes fill me. Ashes of burnt trees, of dead love.

'She says you have failed her,' Game-Servant tells me quietly, her lips close to my ear, her hand on my back. 'She says you have lied to her, you have deceived her, and she no longer wants to learn from you. I am beyond regretful that I am the one who must tell you this.'

'I do not believe you can hear her! Why do you fabricate such lies? Do you not see I am in terrible pain?'

'I am Teacher-Servant now,' she says. 'Nuala has decreed it. I have only to receive the gift of the first gaze.' She Who Was Game-Servant stands tall, and Nuala turns her eyes toward the young woman. As I watch, she is shot through with an invisible beam of ardour. Nuala is bestowing the gift of the first gaze upon the new Teacher-Servant before my very eyes. My cruelty is a child's plaything next to the violence of hers.

She Who Was Game-Servant is transformed before me. She radiates a deep, serene calm. But it turns to a guttural scream as Nuala's thoughts and love pound into her body unchecked.

'You are the holder of this pain now,' I say, standing over her as she crumbles under the bombardment of Nuala's mind. 'I am finally free. I wish you joy.' I grit my teeth and whisper through them, 'And may your joy be trebled in the Service.' I walk away, as tall as my empty legs will allow, leaving Teacher-Servant on her knees. Servants rush to her sides to assist her, not seeing me in their hurry to help the new Teacher-Servant. She does not need me.

Every

Servant and every available citizen has been dispatched to the burning woods at the cemetery. They carry water in whatever vessels are to hand. I tucked myself away and watched for some time, to be sure that the trees—most especially the tree to which Nuala feels closest—were burned to skeletons before the citizenry could become aware. The trees cannot be saved. Their blackened spines will be cut down.

I lent my help for a few minutes, my face a mirror of the fear and confusion of my fellow Servants. When I left the conflagration, I did not go to Nuala. Instead, I watched from my hidden place in the bare bushes some distance away as the great fire consumed the most vocal of the trees, the one with whom Nuala spoke most frequently. Its needles popping and turning to ash, its limbs ablaze, it reached to the sky for the water that would not come. All was clear above me. There would be no rain to help. Fire is part of the natural order. Things of wood are meant to burn. This is their gift both to themselves and to us.

When I return, I steal into the room where Nuala sleeps. I whisper her the Two Great Secrets, though she knows them. She has told me herself. I open my mind until I am sure they have penetrated hers. When I am certain that she is dreaming of them, and what they mean for her, I kiss her for the last time upon her sleeping mouth. I rest my face against her upper lip for a long moment.

I leave her sleeping and walk back in darkness to my small house in the narrow street, my heart tight and splintered, my mind clear, free, my own—just as I had wished—and utterly desolate, the orange glow of the fire piercing the last of the night sky.

In the dim, grey dawn, I remove my Teacher-Servant tunic and hang it in the small closet from which an Iron-Servant will collect it in the morning. I finger the new uniform of the Kitchen-Servant. When the sun rises, I will begin my duties washing and drying the great platters from which the Servants are fed three times daily. The new uniform I will wear when I make the pots of hot tea for Senior Iron-Servant and her staff as they ready Nuala's dress for the day.

There is no longer she and I. She is not mine, and I am not hers.

I have aged ten years in the last few days of learning my new role away from Nuala's eyes. I move through the training without thought or emotion, my insides wooden. Bits of my shredded heart left in the locks tickling the back of her neck. My tangled love wrapped around the Engine's piercing arm. From my frosted window over the sink I can see Teacher-Servant, her strong thighs against Nuala's shoulder, a book in her hands. She reads to Nuala, and though Seeing-Servant is not close by, the little one's eyes close with pleasure.

I—who was Teacher-Servant—watch from a faraway place so that Nuala will not see me, though it would not matter if she did. By her own choosing, I am now a nameless Kitchen-Servant, unworthy of her gaze. When will Nuala learn of the fire? They cannot keep it from her forever.

Now Teacher-Servant climbs down from Nuala's shoulder and spells words I cannot see on the great word board at the foot of her napping chair. She glides from square to square, spelling words, making stories.

I would like to stab out my eyes.

My heart is a cracked and bleeding shell. I cannot think how it continues to keep me alive without Nuala's gaze, the stories she told only me. The love she gave only to me. Part of my heart keeps beating, a pumping of meat, continuing its function to spite me.

I set the great pot to boil and steep the Servants' evening tea.

THE END

ACKNOWLEDGEMENTS

With much affection and gratitude for their invaluable contributions to this work: Gail Anderson-Dargatz, Holly Borgerson Calder, Rebecca Campbell, Myrl Coulter, Joan Crate, Barry Dempster, David Elias, Heidi Greco, Serge Gingras, Leslie Greentree, Catherine Greenwood, Shawna Lemay, Jonathan Meakin, Blaine Newton, and Paul Wharton. To my friends and families everywhere: thank you.

In Liverpool: Justine, Kerry Lo, and Matt. Thank you for sharing your puppeteer stories with me.

In Sfakia (The Trickster and the Muse Workshop and Retreat, 2012): Τα κορίτσια μου: My retreat partner, Lorri Neilsen Glenn, and participants Sally Babie, Jan Barkhouse, Cynthia French, Lekkie Hopkins, Kirsten Koza, and Robyne Wilock.

Our Greek friends and hosts across the south of Crete where Nuala took her first steps: Γιώργος Βοτζάκις, Tsetsa Kaveldjieva, Χρησούλα Νικηφοράκι, και όλους τους φίλους, την οικογένειά μας, και τα παιδιά εκεί.

The Sage Ones (Sage Hill Writing Experience, 2013): Madhur Anand, Heidi Garnett, Katia Grubisic, dee Hobsbawn-Smith, Ella Johnson, Henry Rappaport, Angeline Schellenberg, Kevin Spenst, and Kathleen Wall. Thank you, Philip Adams, MCS, from your HLC.

My deepest thanks to everyone at The University of Alberta Press: Linda Cameron, Cathie Crooks, Alan Brownoff, Monika Igali, Sharon Wilson, Basia Kowal, Mary Lou Roy, and Duncan Turner. I also acknowledge the Alberta Foundation for the Arts and St. Peter's Abbey for the gifts of time and a place to revise this book. Thank you to Carole Baldock at *Orbis: Quarterly International Literary Journal* (#175, UK) for publishing an excerpt and canadianpoetries.com for posting a very early draft.

Don McKay: Thank you for sending me to my room and for telling me to find the novel *Nuala* was asking to be. You helped me to build her, and to teach her to walk.

Helen Moffett: Lady M, you are a rare and precious gem among editors. Your instant commitment to *Nuala* after hearing me read from her for four minutes was nothing short of miraculous. You've helped me polish this wood to a fine, fragrant gleam. Thank you for the long phone calls across the miles that separate Canada and South Africa.

Peter Midgley: Since she was six paragraphs long, you've believed in Nuala, you've fought for her, and you've never left her side. Thank you for many hours of inspiration, conversation, encouragement, and for sending me away to rewrite the whole thing from scratch. You were so right. You are—and always have been—Nuala's champion.

First, last, and always: to my Stu. For sharing my love of giant puppets, and for sharing your life with me.

Other Titles from The University of Alberta Press

THE LAST TEMPTATION OF BOND

KIMMY BEACH

Poet Kimmy Beach has succeeded where
every Bond villain has failed: to kill 007.

YOU HAVEN'T CHANGED A BIT

Stories

ASTRID BLODGETT

Full-fledged characters positively crackle in
the deliciously realistic situations of these
thirteen short stories.

BELIEVING IS NOT THE SAME AS BEING SAVED

LISA MARTIN

Lyric poems that tenderly meditate on life
and death, joy and sorrow, faith and doubt.

More information at www.uap.ualberta.ca